ZOMBIE APOCALYPSE

THE

ORIGIN

Michael K. Clancy

Lyons McNamara LLC

This is a work of fiction. Names, characters, places, and incidents are either the product of the author's imagination or are used fictitiously. Any resemblance to actual persons, living or dead, events or locales is entirely coincidental.

Copyright © 2020 by Janet M. Tavakoli. All rights reserved.

Published by Lyons McNamara LLC, Chicago, Illinois.

No part of this publication may be reproduced, stored in a retrieved system, or transmitted in any form or by any means, electronic, mechanical, photocopying, recording, scanning, or otherwise, except as permitted under Section 107 or 108 of the 1976 United States Copyright Act, without either the prior written permission of the Publisher or authorization through payment of the appropriate per-copy fee to the Publisher.

ISBN 10: 1-943543-20-8
ISBN-13: 9781943543205

Contents

Book 1
HOW I STARTED THE ZOMBIE APOCALYPSE — 7

The Confession of Dr. David Kohlberg 7
    "My best work was top secret." — 7

Washington D.C. Fifteen Hours Later 51
    "Do You Know How He Died?" — 51

CNN Exclusive: Z-Factor Update 60
    BREAKING NEWS — 60

Book 2
ZOMBIE PROTOCOLS — 63

Flatlined 63
    Day Two VA Medical Center Washington, D.C. — 63

Out of Time 70
    Day Two Georgetown Universit Medical Center Washington, D.C. — 70

OODA Loop **77**
    Day Two VA Medical Center Washington, D.C.   **77**

Preparations **97**
    Day Two Georgetown University
    Medical Center Washington, D.C.   **97**

The White House **102**
    Day Two Washington, D.C.   **102**

Evacuation **110**
    Day Two VA Medical Center Washington, D.C.   **110**

Book 3
ZOMBIE CONTAGION   **118**

Anomalies **118**
    Day Four Outbreak Compound, Virginia   **118**

Bitten **137**
    Month Four Homewood Compound   **137**

Ancestors **167**
    Outbreak Compound, Virginia   **167**

Inheritance **170**
    Homewood Compound   **170**

Book 4

ZOMBIES AND MEN **187**

Volunteers 187
    Outbreak Compound, Virginia
    Two Hours Earlier   187

The Chopper 197
    Road from Homewood to the
    Outbreak Compound   197

Special Excerpt from
Zombie Apocalypse 2: WILDFIRE   **235**

You've finished. Before you go… 255
Books by Michael K. Clancy 257
About Michael K. Clancy 259

Book 1

HOW I STARTED THE ZOMBIE APOCALYPSE

The Confession of Dr. David Kohlberg

"My best work was top secret."

IN RESPONSE to the recent outbreak of Ebola in Liberia, followed by the death of an infected German traveler who returned to Berlin, world governments made a rare, bold, united move. Yesterday at 6:00 a.m. London time (8:00 a.m. Tel Aviv time), they began to continuously release my immunizing super virus in every major airport on the globe.

Yesterday at 1:00 p.m. Tel Aviv time (11:00 a.m. London time), Dr. Baruch Lieber and I took a frantic conference call from the commander of the brigade from which six of our ten test subjects came. He holds a rank in the Israel Defense Forces equivalent to a colonel in the U.S. Army. His name is Jonah Weiss. Colonel Weiss reported the death of one of our super virus test subjects.

"Dr. Kohlberg and Dr. Lieber?"

"Yes, we are both here on speakerphone. This is Dr. Kohlberg. I head the team."

I heard a commotion in the background. Anxious voices fired questions at Weiss.

Colonel Weiss raised his voice. "Chief Private Ari Munwes was stabbed in a terror attack near a south Tel Aviv train station. He died of his wounds. *What did you do to him?* All hell is breaking loose in my ranks."

Dr. Lieber and I looked at each other in confusion. We were at a loss to understand Colonel Weiss. I knew Chief Private Munwes well, and I was very fond of him. Quick mind. Wicked sense of humor. I was distressed to hear he had been stabbed, but what did that have to do with us?

"What do you mean?" I asked.

"The soldiers reported...they said Munwes arose from the dead and attacked a fellow soldier. It happened while they were transporting the body to the morgue."

Colonel Weiss's report was utter nonsense. I didn't try to hide my annoyance. "Is this a joke?"

The colonel threw it back at me in spades, and his voice rose to a shout. "*This is no joke. I am telling you what my soldiers told me.*"

This time, Dr. Baruch Lieber and I looked at each other in alarm. Surely, Ari Munwes did not die from his wounds. He must have passed out. But that wouldn't explain why he would attack another soldier. Was this an unanticipated complication of the vaccine, and if so, what exactly was happening? I needed a lot more information.

"How are the soldiers now? How is Ari Munwes doing? What about the soldier that Ari attacked? Is he all right? What about the terrorist?" I kept my voice steady and calm, hoping Weiss would follow my lead.

"I told you. Chief Private Ari Munwes died of stab wounds. There is no room for doubt. It was a vicious attack. He was stabbed through the heart and sliced through his carotid artery, a quarter of the way through his neck. Then, he was stabbed through the throat. He bled out. The terrorist is unharmed and in custody; we are questioning him now."

I took a deep breath and tried to collect my thoughts. For now, I had to suspend disbelief and listen to what the colonel had to say.

"How is the soldier doing...the one Private Munwes attacked?"

The colonel's words spilled out in a rush. "Not well. Private Munwes, or at least what used to be Munwes, *ate* the soldier's left arm. The soldier, Chief Private Danny Fisher, could not fend him off. Munwes ripped through the cloth of Fisher's shirt with his teeth, and he tore chunks out of Fisher's left triceps. Two more soldiers pulled Munwes off Fisher, but Munwes kept lunging at them."

"Did they shoot Munwes?" I asked.

"No. The soldiers didn't want to use bullets in such close quarters. These men are strong and well-trained in hand-to-hand combat. Yet Munwes didn't stop even when they applied pressure to nerves, shattered a knee, and twisted an arm out of its joint."

"If they didn't shoot him, how did they subdue Munwes?"

"They bashed in his head."

I said nothing for a full fifteen seconds. Finally, I asked, "Where is Fisher, the soldier Munwes bit?"

"You mean the soldier he partially ate," said Weiss. "Fisher and Munwes's corpse are on their way to you. I saw Fisher's arm. Shredded, hanging flesh. It looked like he had been mauled by an animal. But worse. It looks ugly. Perhaps infected. Puffy and unhealthy. He's lost a lot of blood, and medics are trying to stabilize him."

I tried to overcome my shock. After the immunizations, we had the test-subject soldiers monitored in what we thought was an abundance of caution. The military had instructions to contact us immediately with any medical problems. We had been thinking in terms of Ebola symptoms, not of even more horrific unintended consequences. What could have caused this?

"Colonel Weiss, I commend the military's quick response time in alerting us. We cannot be sure this is related to the vaccine, but we'll get to the bottom of it. We would like toxicology to examine the blade the terrorist used to stab Chief Private Ari Munwes."

"Yes," said Colonel Weiss, "I didn't mean to jump to conclusions." He paused. "Doctor Kohlberg?"

"Yes, is there something more?"

"There's a lot more. My men are halfway to panic. You'll recall I have five other test subjects in my battalion, and the other men are now saying they don't want to work with them. I need to maintain discipline..."

"As soon as I know more, you will too, Colonel Weiss."

"Thank you," said Colonel Weiss, sounding a little calmer. "And Dr. Kohlberg?"

"Yes?"

"If Chief Private Danny Fisher doesn't make it...be careful."

MY NAME is Dr. David Kohlberg. I was born in Warsaw, Poland, on January 16, 1921. I am an epidemiologist. My trial and conviction for espionage were widely publicized in 2001. Before my arrest, I studied diseases in pre-defined populations. Most of you may be familiar with how scientists study the causes and infection patterns of the flu, AIDs, West Nile fever, and Ebola. After World War II, I made significant contributions to these fields and created new policies for uncovering risk factors and preventative healthcare. Those weren't my most significant contributions, but they were the ones I was allowed to make public.

My best work was top-secret. I developed new weapons for biological warfare for the Israeli military. I studied the effects of biological weapons on populations when our enemies used them on their own citizens. I had top-secret clearance in every country in the European Union, the United States, Israel, and Russia. The reason for the latter clearance is that I was also a spy for the Soviet Union. During the Cold War, I managed smallpox strains for potential germ warfare. I made sure both sides had the same information. After the Soviet Union crumbled, I spied for Russia. I worked on viruses, bacteria, and chemical weapons. I shared that information with Russia, too.

I was simply trying to shift the balance of power so that it did not chiefly reside in only one country. When the USA and Israel temporarily made me disappear, rumors spread, and it tantalized world leaders. When I made my big mistake, everyone wanted to participate. It is important to me that you know how I started my research.

WHEN WORLD WAR II broke out, my father pleaded with me to flee Poland, "*You must take precautions. I want you to stay alive.*" I only half believed his warnings. We were Jewish. My father, my mother, and three younger brothers attended a synagogue, but I had no time for religion. I was eighteen and having a ball.

My best friend was Baruch Lieber, and we had many friends among our fellow students. We spent Sunday evenings in coffee shops dismissing the vague dark rumblings of doom coming from Germany. We talked about science instead. I studied medicine at the University of Warsaw. I was three years younger than my classmates, a prodigy, and I was first in my class.

I was tall and dark, and several girls called me handsome. I loved music and dancing. And I loved Viv, Aviva Goren to her parents. Viv was seventeen. Her large brown eyes brimmed with tears when I told her my father's plans for me. We spent our evenings huddled in intense conversation. She begged me to take her with me if it came to that. She wanted to face the future together. We both knew we were too young for marriage. I couldn't take her with me. I had no money, nothing to offer her but my wits. I held Viv tight and promised that if my father ordered me to leave, I would return for her.

My father relentlessly urged me to go. He thought the men might be in danger, but surely the women would be spared, especially young and beautiful women like Viv. I resisted him. The horror of what was to come was still only a trickle of what I thought were hysterical stories. Jews were beaten and robbed. Some disappeared. Rumors and stories, or so I thought.

After several months—and only after our cousins in Berlin were arrested—I gave in. Viv was inconsolable. She buried her head in my chest and wept thick tears as I stroked her long brown hair.

My father and I argued until the end. I thought he was an alarmist, and I did not hide my exasperation. The look of abject terror in my father's eyes as I bade him farewell haunts me every day. In the years that followed, I bitterly regretted my skepticism.

I reluctantly fled Poland for Russia in the middle of July 1939. I can no longer remember the exact date. I traveled to Minsk, where I completed my medical studies in record time, but it wasn't fast enough.

On September 1, 1939, the Nazis marched into Poland. Two months later, the Germans ordered Jewish Poles to wear white armbands with a blue Star of David. In 1941, Germans standardized the insignias for all Jews in German-occupied territories. Jews were compelled to wear yellow Star of David badges.

In the spring of 1941, the Gestapo's henchmen frog marched my family from our home and forced them to board a transport with no word of the destination. The arrests were part of Operation Reinhard and the Final Solution, a Nazi plan to kill all Jews and other so-called undesirables.

Baruch Lieber witnessed my family's arrest and got word to me through our tight network of friends. The Gestapo was looking for him, too, and he let me know he would try to escape to the United States. But he sent no news about Viv.

Returning home would have meant arrest and a short, brutal life in a concentration camp. I buried my grief in my studies and resolved to work with the Russians against the Nazis. On June 22, 1941, Hitler unleashed Operation

Zombie Apocalypse: The Origin

Barbarossa, the largest of all the German military operations of World War II, the massive invasion of the Soviet Union. The same day, I volunteered to serve in the Red Army Medical Corps.

I served on the front lines for several months. I was a doctor, and I was also a soldier. I finally had a chance to fight back. I killed twenty-six Nazis before shrapnel damaged my left shoulder.

After I recovered, I headed an anti-epidemic army unit at a base camp near the Urals. My enemies were the Germans, dysentery, typhus, typhoid fever, gangrene, pneumonia, tuberculosis, whooping cough, chicken pox, mumps, measles, scarlet fever, malnutrition, and Russian winters. Disease, filth, hunger, and death surrounded me for the rest of the war.

I wasn't in a German concentration camp, but I lived in another kind of death camp. Even though it wasn't surrounded by barbed wire, there was no escape. We had nothing to fight a virus. Our small supply of sulfanilamide was our only antibiotic to treat wounds. The United States wouldn't mass produce penicillin until 1943, and even then, I had no access to it.

Dysentery and typhus were the biggest killers. Dysentery killed by dehydrating its victims. Soldiers suffered paralyzing cramps followed by vomiting and diarrhea mixed with mucous and blood. We soon ran out of intravenous fluids to rehydrate the sick. Prevention was vital. We couldn't always boil enough water, but we could still fight dysentery by digging latrines away from the stream, our main water supply. We hauled garbage to a large dump away from camp.

Of all the diseases, I hated typhus the most. Soldiers were covered with too much grime, and body lice infested every camp. In 1909, Charles Nicolle discovered that lice were a vector for Rickettsia prowazekii, the typhus bacteria. In other words, lice spread typhus. Other scientists proved that lice bites were not the problem; the bacteria spread from lice excrement.

I took care of Private Pavel Alexandrov myself. Pavel's typhus infection started when a louse bite became contaminated with excrement that contained Rickettsial particles. For two days, he felt ill and lethargic. Next, he complained of blinding headaches. His fever rose. An intense rash spread on his body. He had abdominal pain and couldn't eat. He vomited until he had nothing left in his stomach, and then he threw up greenish-yellow bile. His diarrhea started out watery, but after Pavel became dehydrated, his stool turned black and looked like tar. He developed tachycardia; his heart rate became irregular. After two weeks of suffering, Pavel died in a state of delirium. I resolved that a Russian soldier would never suffer that way again if I could help it.

I fought typhus using a dangerous technique developed in Poland in the 1920s by Rudolph Weigl. Lice feed on blood, and Weigl found that the vaccine was most effective if lice fed on *human* blood. I raised lice, infected them with typhus, crushed them into a paste, and made a vaccine. I vaccinated myself and my team, and we made more vaccines for the soldiers.

This method posed only minor problems. It was impossible to completely contain the lice, and the vaccination wasn't perfect. My team became infected, too. They got mildly ill but were in no danger of dying. I felt I had cheated death.

Decades later, my hubris contributed to my big mistake. But I didn't spend time worrying about hubris then. I desperately needed large quantities of typhus vaccine, and I was willing to do whatever it took to get it.

At first, I used wounded and dying Russian volunteers as a source of blood for the lice in the typhus experiments. They were patriots and heroes. Every one of them. But they soon died of their wounds—not typhus—and dead men were of no use to me. I grew impatient. I infected healthy German prisoners of war with typhus and used them as a human blood source. Many of my German prisoners died of typhus, a hideous death.

I took a morally repugnant shortcut, and I did it simply because it was faster and easier for me. I quietly developed vaccines that saved tens of thousands of lives. I tried not to think about the German lives I unnecessarily destroyed in the process.

Official statistics on Russian war casualties stated that 8.7 million Soviet soldiers had died, but the medical community thought it was more like 11 million. Those numbers didn't include nearly 10 million civilians killed by the Nazi's aggressive actions and another 8.6

million civilians who died from disease and famine. Altogether, the Soviet Union lost around 16% of its citizens, or around 27 million people.

After the war, I returned to Poland and learned of my family's fate. My parents and my three younger brothers perished in the Treblinka extermination camp. The Germans had taken Viv, too. They all met their end in Treblinka's gas chambers.

I never had the chance to tell my father how right he had been and how sorry I was for doubting him. I left without telling him I loved him. I had thought him weak and cowardly. Now I realized he was strong. Strong enough to admit to himself that he faced mortal danger and that it frightened him. My father had saved me, and I hoped that in his final days, the thought gave him a small measure of relief from his suffering and terror.

There was nothing left for me in Poland. I immigrated to Israel and worked in a top-secret chemical and biological weapons laboratory near Tel Aviv, a small, growing jewel of a city on the Mediterranean Sea. No one I loved was with me to see the beauty of the sun sparkling on the water. I felt no joy and thought only of loss. *I kept my promise. I came back for you, Viv, but I was too late.*

I felt deep gratitude to the Red Army for giving me the chance to fight the monsters that massacred my family and murdered my beloved Viv. I could not bear to think of how they shaved off her lustrous hair, tattooed her arm with a number, and herded her away to be gassed. She was nothing to them and everything to me.

I was determined that if I could help it, so much power would never again be concentrated in the hands of one man. Power corrupts, and absolute power corrupts absolutely. Israel and the United States had knowledge and power. Russia did not, so when a Russian spy handler approached me, I agreed to spy for the Soviet Union.

I WAS ALONE. I was overjoyed when Baruch Lieber wrote me from the United States in 1947. He was now Dr. Lieber and had read one of my research papers. He was delighted to learn I was alive and well in Tel Aviv. We renewed our friendship and corresponded a few times a week. We traveled back and forth from New York to Tel Aviv. Baruch's family became my new family, and even though we were not blood relatives, his entire family called me Uncle David.

When Baruch's son Shelly was born, I flew to the United States for the bris, the infant's circumcision. I attended every major event in their lives. When Shelly's son Benjamin was born, I attended his milestone events too, at least all that I was at liberty to attend. I was so proud when he graduated with the highest honors from medical school. Benjamin said he studied epidemiology because he was inspired by my research. He became Dr. Benjamin Lieber, the top scientist in the field in the United States.

Meanwhile, my friend Baruch and I co-authored research papers on new flu vaccines. We became even closer. We were the only survivors from our youth in Warsaw. Both of us worked on top-secret biological weapons projects. I worked for Israel, and he worked for the United States. Our governments were allies, and we often performed joint research. I told Baruch more than I should have, but I didn't tell him everything. I didn't tell him about the Russians.

When I had research to pass to the Soviet Union, I set up a meeting with my handler by writing a code in chalk on the outer wall of a pre-agreed Tel Aviv building. I met with him in the back room of a Russian Orthodox Church. As we drank vodka and ate caviar, I explained the fine points of the research. The Russians awarded me the Red Banner of Labor, the second-highest honor in the Soviet Union.

I never thought of myself as a spy. I never took a penny for my work. I did it because I thought it was the right thing to do. Weapons had to be shared. Otherwise, the strongest nation inevitably becomes a bully. It is dangerous to have an imbalance in scientific knowledge. Or so I told myself. I thought I was preventing fascism.

YESTERDAY, in Tel Aviv, I was reminded of Private Pavel Alexandrov. His suffering from typhus seemed less horrifying than what I saw when medics brought in Chief Private Danny Fisher, the soldier who was bitten by Munwes. By the time he arrived at our facility, Fisher was running a high fever. We kept him in isolation. His ragged wound looked puffy and infected. It oozed slime, and I recoiled at the noxious odor. We took samples for analysis. Even a superbug, a flesh-eating bacteria, couldn't cause so much damage or look this unwholesome this fast.

My staff transfused and hydrated Fisher. They started antivirals and antibiotics. But Fisher kept failing, and we were shooting in the dark. Fisher's fever and the condition of the wound suggested rapid infection and a strong and perhaps counterproductive hyper-aggressive immune system response.

We restrained him so that if he died, his potential reanimation would not become a threat. We hoped against hope that any possibility of reanimation—if that is what it was—ended with Munwes. I hoped Fisher would either recover or die, but either way, that would be the end of it. Nonetheless, as a precaution, we tied down his ankles and wrists and used a chest restraint and a head restraint. We immobilized Fisher's head using a wide band across the forehead. We posted security surveillance and created a perimeter.

In the beginning, Fisher was conscious and frightened. I wanted to know more about Munwes's attack, and I asked him what he recalled. His fever was high, but he was still lucid.

"He was dead. Just lying there. I had my back to him, and I was facing the soldiers at the rear of the transport, blocking their view of Munwes. I felt something brush against my back, and then I felt and heard the cloth of my sleeve tearing. I wasn't scared, just confused. He was dead, right? I turned around, and he clamped onto the back of my arm, ripped off a chunk of flesh and swallowed it in one gulp. Then he clamped down again. I twisted around and tried to use my right hand to push back his forehead, but he was too strong. He just wouldn't stop."

Fisher's eyes opened wide, and he thrashed against the restraints. He seemed to be reliving the horror.

I tried to soothe him. "You did the best you could. The jaw muscle is the strongest in the body."

"He just wouldn't stop," repeated Fisher. Then, he dropped off into a deep sleep.

Death was near. From the time he arrived, Fisher refused all food and drink. He had no interest in oral nourishment. His blood pressure dropped. He awoke intermittently and seemed disoriented. He no longer seemed to know who was in the room. His veins mottled in a purplish pattern from reduced blood circulation. His breathing grew labored, and phlegm rattled in his throat.

Dr. Baruch Lieber and I were there to witness the end. Baruch pronounced Fisher dead at 6:15 p.m. Tel Aviv time. I felt relieved, but it was short-lived. At 6:23 p.m. Tel Aviv time, Fisher reanimated. He issued guttural moaning sounds, and he made loud chomping sounds as he repeatedly opened his mouth and crashed his upper and lower teeth together. He pulled against the restraints and unsuccessfully tried to turn his head to bite Dr. Lieber.

We wanted to study Fisher, but the military deemed that it wasn't worth risking lives and ended Fisher with a bullet through the left temple.

WHAT went wrong? Over decades, I saved over a million lives with new healthcare protocols and vaccine enhancements for a variety of diseases, including flu and my old enemy, typhus. In the tropics, rat fleas spread murine typhus. It showed up in suburban Texas and California, transmitted by cat fleas. I traveled to Africa to research ways to eradicate it.

My time in Africa led me to study Ebola and other viral hemorrhagic fevers. In case you do not recall, hemorrhagic means abnormal blood flow. I'll get to why that happens in a minute. Even though this group of viruses all causes hemorrhaging, they are all very different.

These viruses use genetic material, ribonucleic acid (RNA), and require a host for survival. Usually, they start with an insect host or an animal host, and from there, they sometimes spread to humans. Some, but not all, can be spread human-to-human. Usually, but not always, that requires contact of some sort. Some viruses are airborne. Fortunately, even airborne viruses are usually restricted to where the hosts live, or at least that used to be true.

All these viruses are unpredictable, and some are deadly. Lassa fever is an arenavirus and is usually transmitted by rodent excrement. The most dreaded of these viruses are the filoviruses like Ebola, which spreads when humans come in contact with an infected person's blood, mucous, and waste. Ebola only rarely becomes airborne.

Ebola is particularly nasty. I autopsied several victims. The virus doesn't kill an infected person. The patient's immune system attempts to kill the virus and goes into a cytokine storm. The patient kills himself. The worst strains have a 90% kill rate, and it is an ugly death.

Every time I opened the corpse of an Ebola victim, it looked as if the body were eating itself from the inside out. A lot of tissue died before the patient did. From the smallest cell to the largest clump of tissue, the body looked as if it consumed itself from the inside out. Organs liquefied. The liver, kidneys, and brain looked like Jell-O.

The blood vessels became permeable, and nitric oxide made the blood thinner. Before death, the patients' blood pressures plummeted because veins and capillaries leaked plasma and blood. Patients oozed blood from the nose, ears, eyes, and even fingernails.

My microscopic examination was even more horrifying. Worse than HIV. Ebola stopped the immune system from making antibodies. The virus ran wild. Multiple viruses invaded a single cell. Cells died and exploded.

I thought I knew a way to mutate Ebola so that humans could only transfer the virus via saliva, and only if saliva entered the bloodstream. That would stop the rapid spread. Humans do not usually run around biting each other, especially when they are dying of hemorrhagic fever. Humans would have to stop kissing infected people and stop sharing utensils and cups. Even so, Ebola would be much easier to manage.

The Israeli government did not view Ebola as a threat, so it would not fund my research. Instead, the government gave me money to fight flu viruses, so I began work on them.

My research was top-secret. My original handler died of natural causes, and I had a new young handler, Anton Abelev. I shared all my research and ideas with him, and he shared Russian research with me. As my research progressed and became more exciting, I met with Abelev more often.

After one of my meetings with Abelev, I walked home down Disengoff Avenue in Tel Aviv and ran smack into Dr. Baruch Lieber. We had dinner and talked all night. We both hated fascism. I decided to recruit him for my information-sharing cause, and I eventually introduced him to Anton Abelev.

Baruch was genuinely surprised when I explained I was spying for the Russians, but he was easily persuaded. Looking back, it was too easy, and he was too eager. But I was not paying close attention. I was excited by my new ideas, and I was sure I had a cure for a nasty flu strain. That was why I did not suspect that Baruch was a double agent working for the United States and cooperating with Mossad.

Mossad, Israeli intelligence, had been mildly suspicious of me for years, but only because I had been an officer in the Red Army. They contacted their American allies and recruited Baruch to keep a casual eye on me. After decades of surveillance, no one suspected I was a spy. There was no money trail to follow. If I had not confided in Baruch, they would still be in the dark.

We persuaded our governments to collaborate and supply more funds to our new project, and Baruch was assigned to work with me. Whatever I came up with, I wanted it to work 100% of the time. If I ran a test with a small rat population, I wanted a Z-Factor of 1.0, a perfect score. Our top-secret research was code-named Z-Factor.

OUR first task was to create a virus, an *immunizing super virus*, to stop a flu virus strain. For three years, we worked day and night on nothing else. We invented a powerful new method to create new viruses for a new type of flu vaccine, one that would be effective against a rapidly mutating flu virus. This had never been done before and was a groundbreaking achievement. The new flu vaccine could be administered by manual injection. I shared the information with Anton Abelev.

The following year, we perfected an *airborne* super virus flu vaccine to combat a new deadly strain of flu. We used a fresh batch of lab rats for the test, and the experiment exceeded our expectations on every level. The airborne super virus had an extraordinary affinity for living cells. The rats remained healthy, and they were immune to the targeted flu strain. We manually vaccinated our entire team and got the same result.

Dr. Baruch Lieber and I were elated and awed by the potential of our discovery. We asked for ten healthy human volunteers from the Israeli army. By placing each of the ten soldiers farther from the airborne immunization source, we tested the range of the super virus.

We started with 100 meters, a little over 328 feet. By the time we got to the tenth soldier, we had constructed a twenty-mile-long airtight tunnel with the soldier on one end and the immunizing super virus on the other. The airborne super viruses seemed to seek out the soldier's living cells like guided missiles. The range seemed unlimited. Each of the soldiers was immunized against the flu strain, and there were no side effects, or so we thought.

Prior to the airborne tests, there was no human-to-human super virus immunization. But the soldiers we immunized with the hyper-aggressive airborne super virus vaccine were different. They were the vector, an extremely powerful vector. Once they left our airtight facility, they infected everyone. The immunizing super virus leaped around the globe almost instantaneously. The airborne super virus delivery system did not discriminate; it immunized every human who was alive.

We were worried, but we asked ourselves how worried we should be. Was it so bad that we had inadvertently unleashed an immunizing super virus that protected Earth's entire human population from a deadly strain of flu virus? We got lucky.

Our research had tremendous potential as an immunization delivery mechanism, but it also had tremendous potential for biological warfare. Our governments ruled it too dangerous to repeat our experiments. The super virus delivery mechanism had great potential to heal, but it also had great potential to spread misery.

I wanted to share the instantaneous global delivery mechanism with Anton Abelev. No one would ever abuse this, I reasoned. If it were used for harmful purposes, everyone would be harmed. No one would be insane enough to do that. I had already shared my hybrid virus engineering research with the Russians, and I felt there was no downside to giving them the mechanism for instantaneous global immunization.

I made my way to the pre-agreed building wall. I pulled out my chalk and wrote a coded message for Abelev. The instant I finished, Israeli military officers took me into custody. I was convicted of espionage. The instantaneous global delivery mechanism was deemed so potentially dangerous that the Israeli government made me disappear. They gave me a new false identity and imprisoned me in Ashkelon. I was sentenced to the maximum sentence of twenty years, and I served ten of those years in solitary confinement.

Dr. Baruch Lieber stuck his neck out for me, arguing that I was misguided but not malicious. I like to think Baruch's intercession is the reason I wasn't executed in secret. But it is possible that our governments did not want to destroy me in case I could be useful again.

Ten years in solitary confinement is a long time. I was not given access to a laboratory or equipment of any kind, but I was allowed writing and reading materials. I spent the time working on a cure for Ebola, even though I had no way to test my theories. When I was moved from solitary confinement to the general prison population, I was allowed to share my research with the Israeli government's biological warfare scientists. They, in turn, shared the information with the Americans, including Dr. Baruch Lieber. I do not know what Israel got in exchange for that information. Even with my research in hand, developing an Ebola vaccine would not be easy.

During the years I was in prison, my friend Baruch won the Nobel Prize for our eradication of the aggressive flu strain for which we had created the super virus vaccine. Our work had been top-secret at the time, but given its success, our governments declassified the information on how we created the vaccine. They kept our method of hyper-aggressive instantaneous global airborne delivery secret.

The United States claimed that the immunization was included in the next batch of annual flu shots. But Asian and European scientists disproved it. The media ignored them and repeated Washington's talking points.

Of course, I was still secretly held in prison, and I got no public credit for the research. Dr. Baruch Lieber collected the Nobel Prize alone. Baruch said he wished I could have claimed the honor with him, and he put aside half of the prize money for me. I thought he was more than generous. My secret imprisonment was not his fault.

My old Russian friends told their allies there was more to the story: a new airborne delivery system. I had disappeared, and they knew there was a cover-up. Stories spread like wildfire. World governments were tantalized. India, China, Japan—everyone wanted to get their hands on the research. They suspected we had perfected an airborne delivery system, but everyone thought it had a wide but limited range. Only the United States and Israel knew the delivery system had a global range.

As the years passed, no one ever again got sick from that particular flu strain. The first thing I asked Baruch when I was allowed out of solitary confinement was whether the passing ten years had revealed any negative consequences of the vaccine. I was relieved that the answer was *none whatsoever*. Our rush to human testing had been my one regret. Now, I felt that the results had been so beneficial that I was vindicated and justified for taking shortcuts.

My Ebola research in solitary confinement shaved a little time off my sentence. Six months ago, the Israeli government released me on parole to work on another top-secret project. At my age, there was no time to waste. The Israeli government wanted a vaccine, or ideally a cure, for Ebola. The virus seemed a remote scare, but the previous outbreak spread to Egypt, Israel's neighbor.

I was overjoyed to have the opportunity to prove my good intentions and to do some good in my nineties, the last days of my life. I repeated my past mistakes and took shortcuts. I slapped together a team in record time. I believed that I was so important and indispensable that other than Baruch, my team members were of secondary importance, and I did not know them well. This time, my shortcuts would have unimaginable consequences.

Baruch and I began work. But this time, instead of a flu virus, we sought a cure for the deadliest strain of Ebola. Our entire team and our host subjects were kept in airtight isolation so there would be no chance of prematurely releasing the new super virus. My prison research gave us a huge head start, and we rapidly advanced. Our tests on our rats were successful. They were immune to the deadliest

Ebola strain with no apparent side effects. A perfect Z-Factor. We repeated the test multiple times, with the same result each time.

Our laboratory uses a humane method to euthanize test rodents after we complete a trial. We have them inhale an anesthetic—we use isoflurane—before gassing them with carbon dioxide. All our test rats, including the rats used in our most recent immunization studies, died by this method. The rats died, and the rats stayed dead.

Ten courageous Israeli army volunteers, five men and five women, agreed to let us expose them to the immunizing super virus. Chief Private Ari Munwes was one of the volunteers. The result was that all of them were immune to the Ebola strain.

Our research appeared to be a complete success. Yet it would all go horribly wrong. We had no warning of what was to come.

YOU might be wondering why world governments decided to release the super virus vaccine in major airports. After all, it was unnecessary; the airborne super virus would instantaneously immunize the planet.

The reason is that we lied to world leaders. We told them the super virus vaccine was airborne, but it had a limited range. We explained that the humans we vaccinated in airports would spread the immunization to everyone who had contact with them. These newly immunized contacts would spread the vaccine even further. Anyone isolated enough to avoid immunization would benefit from herd immunity because the spread of contagion would be contained. That was our cover story to keep other governments in the dark.

The United States and Israel decided to keep the true range of the instantaneous global mechanism secret. Only Dr. Lieber and I knew the range; the rest of my team did not have our level of security clearance. Yet we alone were authorized to manufacture the new airborne super virus vaccine in Tel Aviv.

These decisions were made by top war game theorists from the Pentagon and the Israeli military. I was allowed to attend the final discussion.

These clever men presented their theories, and everything pointed to one course of action. General Hollcroft from the U.S. Army summed it up:

The proprietary super virus delivery system has enormous potential for use in malicious biological warfare. For example, we no longer routinely immunize people against smallpox because the disease has been eradicated. If a megalomaniac grabbed the reins of power of a hostile government, he could manually immunize his own population and then release the smallpox virus around the globe.

It would take decades for infected countries to recover from the devastation. The immunized country would be in a position to take over the world economy, and it would have a superior military advantage.

It *seemed* obvious and correct. No one saw any flaw in the logic. But we did not take into account our old habits and biases.

Intelligence services managed strategic lies and secrets. They planted false information to confound enemies; they pried secrets from others; they killed people to protect state secrets. We imagined a scenario of what could go wrong if we told. But we never asked ourselves what could go wrong *if we did not tell* that our proprietary super virus delivery method would infect everyone on the planet.

EVERYONE was infected. After I learned of Munwes's death and reanimation, I suspected that if one of our test subjects died traumatically, he reanimated. But that's all I suspected around 1:00 p.m. yesterday. I had no way of knowing whether reanimation would happen again or if there were something special about Munwes and the circumstances of his death.

After we took Colonel Weiss's call about Private Danny Fisher's infected bite, in an abundance of caution, we alerted Israel Defense epidemic control to get them to the site of as many deaths as possible as soon as possible.

As Fisher's condition steadily deteriorated, I kept defense forces up to date, but information coming back to me was much slower. When we could not heal Private Danny Fisher, I suspected that if a zombie bit someone, it somehow acted as a catalyst to accelerate illness and death. Those bitten reanimate as zombies. But what happens if someone dies of natural causes? I needed more information. Unfortunately, I had the answer to my question sooner than I thought I would.

After staff moved Fisher's body to the morgue, Baruch returned to his office. The strain of the day's events was too much for him. Apparently, sometime between 6:30 p.m. and 7:05 p.m. Tel Aviv time, my lifelong friend Dr. Baruch Lieber succumbed to a heart attack. At 7:15 p.m. Tel Aviv time, an Israeli soldier entered Baruch's office to remind him about Munwes's autopsy. This is a brief summary of his account.

> "I opened the door, and the room was very dim but not completely dark. Dr. Lieber was not at his desk. I called out his name. No answer. I reached for the light switch. Another hand was already there. A cold hand. Dr. Lieber had been standing in a recess next to the switch. That's why I didn't see him, and when I reached out my hand, he went for it. He grabbed at it, and his head moved quickly toward my hand. I pulled it back

before he could bite me. I gave him a hard kick to the torso, and it moved him back. I flipped the switch, and he made low guttural sounds, exactly like Fisher. His hazy eyes seemed unfocused, and purplish veins lined his face. He gnashed his teeth and came at me again. I ended him with a bullet to the forehead."

We tried to discover the disease's mechanism. We brought Munwes's body to the morgue. I attended the autopsy of our test subject stab-victim soldier performed by Dr. Avram Goldstein, a member of my team and an experienced forensic pathologist. We do not yet know what to make of the results.

It seems there is something about the process of dying: slowing of metabolism, cessation of breathing, reduced oxygen in the bloodstream, combined with chemical changes as organs cease to function, that allows the virus to enter cells and spread. This somehow triggers the reanimation of a part of the brain that controls motor function. There may also be a rapid mutation of the victim's DNA.

¤

DR. AVRAM GOLDSTEIN seemed on the edge of a nervous breakdown. He stared in disbelief at his own findings after Munwes's autopsy. His eyes were wide and bulging, and he kept saying *no, no, no*. I soon discovered the reason for his distress.

Colonel Jonah Weiss marched into our facility accompanied by six of his unit's soldiers. At first, I thought Weiss had suffered another fatal casualty in his unit. Two of his men sandwiched Dr. Goldstein between them. They each held one of Goldstein's arms in a vice-like grip. Colonel Weiss had another prisoner with him. It was my former Russian handler, Anton Abelev. Colonel Weiss, Anton Abelev, and Dr. Avram Goldstein looked equally terrified.

"Around 90 minutes ago, we intercepted a communication between Dr. Avram Goldstein and Anton Abelev. I believe you and Mr. Abelev are already acquainted," said Colonel Weiss.

"Yes," I said.

"Are you aware that two days ago, a massive wave of Russian troops mobilized in Ukraine near Kiev?"

"No, I wasn't aware."

Colonel Weiss gave me a hard look.

"Go on, tell him," said Colonel Weiss to Dr. Goldstein.

Weiss chose his target well. The physician lacked Abelev's mental toughness.

"We only meant to infect Kiev," blurted Dr. Goldstein.

I interrupted. "What do you mean you meant to *infect* Kiev? Our tests showed that our virus immunized people against Ebola."

Goldstein moaned. "I substituted a Russian-made virus for the vaccine and merged it with the airborne delivery system prepared for Kiev's Boryspil International Airport. Now there are reports..."

"*Wait*," I said. "You tampered with the vaccine and delivered a harmful virus instead?"

"Yes, that's what I'm trying to tell you," responded Goldstein.

"What kind of virus?" I asked.

Goldstein broke down. "For lack of a better term, they call it a...a zombie virus."

"A *zombie* virus?" I would not have believed him if I had not witnessed the events of the day first-hand.

Goldstein nodded. "That's why Russia mobilized troops. They figured desperate citizens in Kiev would beg them for military intervention. Russia planned to clean out Kiev and take back the Ukraine. But something has gone horribly wrong."

"Yes." It was all I could manage to say. The irony was staggering. If I had *not shared* virus engineering research with Russia, she would not have been able to create the zombie virus. Yet had we *shared* the truth about the delivery system, Russia would never have released the zombie virus, at least not in that way.

Dr. Goldstein continued. "You told us the airborne vaccine had limited range. But there are widespread reports..."

Now, Colonel Weiss interrupted. "Exactly what are we dealing with, Dr. Kohlberg? How bad is it?"

"Russia did not just infect Kiev; Russia infected the entire Ukraine, Russia, and the rest of the planet. Dr. Goldstein married the zombie virus to an instantaneous global delivery mechanism," I explained. There was no point in secrecy anymore.

Colonel Weiss's face was ghostly pale. "Are you saying we are all infected...everyone on this planet?"

"Yes," I responded. "The best we can do now is to try to contain it while we search for a cure."

ISRAEL has only around 8 million people, less than the city of New York. On average, one hundred fourteen people die in Israel every day. Of course, that number varies a lot from day to day. Dealing with this crisis has taken all our manpower and resources. By 1:00 a.m. today, Tel Aviv time, Israel Defense Forces reported yesterday's death toll at one hundred two people, or one hundred two zombies. Each zombie bit one person on average.

Most zombies were killed immediately—before anyone got bitten. When the living got over their shock and realized what the risen were trying to do, they fought back. But other zombies bit multiple victims. We isolated all the victims we were able to find. Yesterday's victims all died and reanimated. We ended them. That doesn't count the people who will die today, and we are not sure we have accounted for all the people who died yesterday.

Zombie Apocalypse: The Origin

I DO NOT know how to stop the virus. I would like to work on a cure. But I am under house arrest. There are guards outside. They do not bother me, and I am allowed to see my lawyer, but I am not allowed to leave.

I have tried to write my confession in layman's terms. I wish to be clear. A pandemic like this has never happened before. The *Russians unleashed a zombie apocalypse, and my research helped them do it.*

Everyone is infected. Everyone who dies will reanimate. The reanimated corpses, the zombies, will seek out living flesh to eat. A zombie bite will cause a viral storm in the bitten victim, who will soon die and reanimate. The only thing that will stop a zombie is to destroy its brain.

Your governments will lie to you. I have seen this first-hand. The bodies of my friend, Dr. Baruch Lieber, and the two infected soldiers were whisked away and burned. Initial reports of reanimations have been suppressed. Governments do not want to admit they have no plan and they cannot control the problem. The powerful and informed will hoard information; they will profiteer and accumulate resources at the expense of the ignorant.

I cannot find the words to express my distress and sorrow, and no apology will ever be good enough. I wish all of you the best of luck.

Zombie Apocalypse: The Origin

Washington D.C. Fifteen Hours Later

"Do You Know How He Died?"

DR. Benjamin Lieber finished reading Uncle David's confession. His tall, muscular body tensed, and he said nothing as his mind raced through the implications. He turned to William Levy, his uncle's lawyer. Benjamin's dark brown eyes held Levy's in a steady gaze.

"You have come a long way to hand-deliver this. Why didn't he use email? Why didn't he call me?" Benjamin asked.

"The military shut down his email accounts. He was not allowed to use the phone; a military liaison fetched me at his request." Levy's voice cracked, and he nervously cleared his throat. "He stayed up all night typing on his computer and printed it out this morning. He hired a private jet and made it stand-ready until he finished. He asked me to personally courier this to you."

"So, he died after you left him."
"Yes."

"You led me to believe my uncle died of natural causes. But now I must ask you. Do you know how he died?"

Levy was taken aback, and he stuttered. "I'm...I'm sorry; I am not at liberty to tell you."

"I am afraid I cannot accept that answer. How did he die?"

Levy didn't answer.

Benjamin rose from his chair. He wasn't trying to intimidate the man, only to meet him on equal terms. But at six feet three inches, he was six inches taller than Levy and a commanding presence.

Levy lowered his eyes, and for the second time, he dodged Benjamin's question. "He gave me this note, and he told me to give it to you after you read his confession." Levy reached into his briefcase and produced a slim white letter-sized envelope. Unlike the bulky confession, the letter was unsealed. His hand shook as he handed it to Benjamin.

"Have you read this?"

Levy's cheeks turned bright red. "The military wouldn't tell me anything, and David was pretty mysterious. But I know this is huge. Troops are mobilizing, and the atmosphere is grim. The note didn't clear things up. Will you tell me what is going on?"

"Tell me how he died."

"They called…they called me just as I was about to board the jet. He grabbed a soldier's side arm and shot himself in the head."

Benjamin slowly nodded and thought. *Yes, that's what I would have done.*

"I am sorry. He was a great man," said Levy with genuine sadness.

Benjamin's eyes glistened, but he shoved aside his grief, straightened his shoulders, and gave Levy a slight nod. "Thank you."

"Will you tell me what is going on? Are we expecting a terrorist attack? A *nuclear* attack?"

Benjamin hesitated. Uncle David wanted him to tell the world. He might as well start with Levy. There were already scattered alarming reports, and there must be a leak. The media was calling the virus Z-Factor.

"I'll tell you. But only after I read his note."

Benjamin opened the envelope's flap and pulled out a single piece of paper. He unfolded it and read the short, hand-written message.

Dearest Benjamin,

My darling boy, it pains me to leave you with this burden. I hope that one day you can find it in your heart not to despise me for what I have done. I know my confession must seem incredible to you, but I assure you I am of sound mind.

Please make my confession public. Try to get people to listen and to prepare themselves. Try to find a cure. But first, heed my warning.

You must take precautions. I want you to stay alive.

All my love,

Uncle David

If anyone else had left this message, Benjamin would not have believed it. But Levy's demeanor, the news of a mysterious Z-Factor virus, today's intelligence about disturbing events at several hospitals, his trust in his uncle, and his life-long knowledge of his uncle's work made it believable.

How much time had passed? Tel Aviv was 7 hours ahead. It was 2:30 p.m. in Washington,

D.C., and Levy left at 5:30 a.m. Tel Aviv time today. He spent 13 or 14 hours in the air on a private jet to Washington, not to mention travel to and from airports.

No, it was better to work backward from the time the virus was released in Kiev. It was released yesterday at 6:00 a.m. London time, which was midnight in Washington D.C. and New York. That was 38 hours ago. There was no time to lose.

Benjamin used his encrypted system to notify the Pentagon and his team that he was initiating emergency outbreak protocols. His uncle's document wasn't classified, at least not yet. It was private correspondence. He scanned it to his hard drive and bolded the key paragraphs about the super virus. He switched to his unencrypted system and emailed Dr. David Kohlberg's confession to his colleagues in the intelligence community, his research colleagues, his wife, the list of 500 doctors and scientists who had attended his last epidemiology conference, and the Surgeon General of the United States. They might not believe it today, but if this developed as rapidly as he thought it would, they would believe him soon enough.

Benjamin printed out twelve hard copies and handed one to Levy. "You'd better take this. You'll want to read it more than once," Benjamin said as he escorted Levy to the door.

"I'll read it on the plane."

"You might want to read it first and then decide," said Benjamin.

The fear returned to Levy's eyes. "Your uncle told me to bring my family. I did. We packed essentials, just in case. My worst fears have come true. We are facing nuclear war."

"No," said Benjamin. "This is worse."

AS SOON as Levy left, Benjamin made three calls. The first was to his wife. He was relieved when she picked up on the first ring.

"Julia, it's me. Do you have the checklist of outbreak protocols handy?"

"Of course. Is this about the Z-Factor virus?"

"Yes."

"An outbreak?"

"Yes."

"I heard on the news that your Uncle David died. I'm so sorry. Does this have something to do with it?"

"Yes, but he didn't die of the virus."

"Can you tell me more?"

"Check your email. Tell Carl to come home from school. Pick him up if you must. Make an excuse. Follow the old protocols. Get Carl to help. Lock up. Doors, windows, the garage, the car. Everything. Set the alarm."

"Ben, you're scaring me. The protocols don't call for lock-down right away."

"I know. I'll make up new protocols later, but for now, follow the old ones. We'll talk later. Love you."

"Love you too. I'm on it."

That's my Julia, he thought. *A good woman in a storm.* He took a deep breath and exhaled. He was glad he wasn't facing this alone. The next few days would make all the difference.

His second call was to the Surgeon General of the United States.

"He's in a meeting and cannot be disturbed," intoned the Surgeon General's assistant as if his call were an annoyance.

Benjamin pulled rank. "This is Dr. Benjamin Lieber of Georgetown University Medical Center and the Pentagon's Pandemic Control Team. I've initiated outbreak protocols. This is not a drill. Interrupt the meeting and bring him a note. Tell him to check his email and have him call me at this number after he's read it."

"But..."

Benjamin was taken aback. Who trained her? The word *but* had no place in this conversation.

"It is a top priority," Benjamin said, using a tone that exuded authority. "And patch me into his voice mail."

Benjamin left a message on the Surgeon General's voice mail and left his number again slowly and clearly.

His third call was to an executive producer at CNN, an old friend. If they were to head this off, the government had to act fast. Thirty-eight hours had already been wasted.

Around 6,775 people die every day in the United States. Most of them die in hospitals, hospices, or other institutions. But people die of car accidents, bullet wounds, drug overdoses, slipping in the bathtub, and any number of odd accidents. Death can happen anywhere.

If 6,775 died yesterday, and each zombie successfully bit and infected one person, on average, then there would have been 13,550 zombies at the start of the day. If there were 6,775 deaths today, and each of yesterday's zombies bit one person today, there would be 20,325 zombies by day's end. That did not count the victims of the people who died today.

By the end of tomorrow, day 3, there would be at least 47,000. By the end of the day after tomorrow, there would be over 101,000. If the zombies infected more than one person per day on average, the numbers would balloon even faster. This had to be brought under control right away.

Benjamin needed to run the numbers, run scenarios, and determine how long it would take before the population would be overwhelmed. But if everyone acted right away, there was a chance for containment.

People had to be warned.

Michael K. Clancy

CNN Exclusive: Z-Factor Update

BREAKING NEWS

Dr. Benjamin Lieber, a noted epidemiologist, revealed he just received important new intelligence about the sudden global outbreak of the new virus known as Z-Factor. Dr. Lieber is the grandson of the late Nobel Prize winner Dr. Baruch Lieber and grandnephew of the late Dr. David Kohlberg, an Israeli epidemiologist.

Dr. Baruch Lieber, 95, died yesterday in Tel Aviv. Dr. David Kohlberg, 95, died earlier today in Tel Aviv. Calls to Israeli authorities to determine the causes of death were not returned. CNN will provide updates as they become available.

Just before he died, Dr. Kohlberg instructed his lawyer to fly via private jet to Washington D.C. and hand-deliver a document to Dr. Benjamin Lieber at Georgetown University's medical research facility. The document purportedly implicates Dr. Kohlberg's top-secret research in the Z-Factor outbreak. The disclosure would have been a violation of the late Dr. Kohlberg's terms of parole.

In 2001, an unidentified double agent working for the United States exposed Dr. Kohlberg as the highest-ranking Soviet spy in history. Under top-secret interrogation, Dr. Kohlberg confessed. An Israeli military tribunal found Dr. Kohlberg guilty of espionage. He received the maximum sentence of 20 years.

Israel believed Dr. Kohlberg's biological weapons research and spying were so dangerous that they created a false identity for Dr. Kohlberg and imprisoned him in secret in the high-security prison known as Ashkelon. Dr. Kohlberg served the first ten years of his sentence in solitary confinement.

Six months ago, the elderly scientist was paroled and released under house arrest with the stipulation that he continue work on a top-secret project but remain silent about his research.

CNN Newsroom will interview Dr. Benjamin Lieber at 7:00 p.m. EST.

CNN Update: Dr. Benjamin Lieber will be unable to appear on *CNN Newsroom* this evening. In his place, we will interview the Surgeon General of the United States, who has just issued a statement that Z-Factor is "self-limiting and contained" and in "no danger" of becoming an epidemic.

Zombie Apocalypse: The Origin

BOOK 2

ZOMBIE PROTOCOLS

Flatlined

Day Two
VA Medical Center Washington, D.C.

"*Come on!*" Grace exclaimed in frustration. Dr. Grace Waters hated losing patients, especially one so young. It was hard to believe a man in his early twenties could so thoroughly destroy his body with drugs and drink.

Grace explained for Jim's and Bill's benefit. Her two brand new interns were having an exciting first day: "The patient was a heroin abuser, among other things. He came into the emergency room earlier today with overdose-induced respiratory failure, which threatened heart failure. The ER gave him Naloxone, an opiate antagonist."

"Not epinephrine?" asked Jim.

"No. In heroin overdoses, Naloxone restarts respiration. Epinephrine doesn't do that. An hour and a half ago, the patient was apparently awake and sober before he was transferred to this room. But the heroin lasted longer than the Naloxone. He stopped breathing again, and this time, his heart stopped. That's when Nurse Inez initiated code blue, summoning my ten-person team."

"What are his chances?" asked Jim.

"Only around 15 percent of patients survive after the heart stops, but he's young. Let's see if he's a fighter. Step in for a closer look."

Grace authorized one of the team to administer another dose of Naloxone directly into the patient's intravenous catheter. She nodded for another to give an additional electrical pulse to the heart. They did CPR for two minutes. "I see signs of a return of spontaneous blood circulation," said Grace.

The patient revived, and then the addict went into instant withdrawal. Angry that his high was gone, he violently attacked Jim. His eyes looked crazed. He bit and scratched and lunged for Jim's throat. He shouted barely intelligible curses at Jim and then threw up all over him. Grace nearly laughed at the shocked look on Jim's face as she and four of her team members dragged the patient off him.

The patient kept fighting them, but they finally subdued him.

Then, the patient convulsed, and his heart began failing again in the middle of a seizure. The patient still had a shockable rhythm. "Again!" Grace nodded to the team member manning the defibrillator. The patient's chest rose with the new shock. The team gave him CPR for two minutes. The patient already had an advanced airway in place. They were losing him, so Grace pulled out the stops. "Epinephrine every 3-5 minutes, and repeat the cycle of shock and CPR," she ordered.

They labored for another 25 minutes. The heart gave a feeble, shockable rhythm after each attempt until, finally, it failed. The patient flatlined.

I might as well give my new interns some practical experience, Grace thought. Aloud, she said, "Step aside, and let's see if the interns learned anything." The team made room, and the interns quickly got into position.

"Let's try epinephrine again. Bill, you administer it."

Bill plunged the needle into the rubber injection disk and emptied the syringe of epinephrine into the IV tube.

"Jim, your turn with the defibrillator." Jim administered another dose of electrical current to the patient's heart. The monitor displayed a flat line.

"Good. Now, two minutes of CPR."

They worked the cycle for another ten minutes: shock, CPR, epinephrine, but the patient stayed flatlined.

Everyone was nearing exhaustion. Almost forty minutes of touch-and-go took its toll.

"That's it," said Dr. Grace Waters. She looked at the clock. "I'm calling it. The patient died at 2:05 p.m."

The team left the room while Grace wrote her notes. Bill and Jim stayed for a debriefing while Inez took inventory of the remaining medications.

Jim hovered over the corpse to clear wires and attachments from its chest. Bill stood on the other side of the bed, helping him. Out of the corner of her eye, Grace saw a swift movement and turned toward the patient. The patient had revived. She froze for a second, horrified. The patient opened his jaws wide, lunged for Jim's neck, and clamped down hard. Jim's scream gave sound to terror and pain.

Blood spurted in all directions.

"Jim!" Bill shouted. From the other side of the bed, he grabbed the patient by the right arm in an attempt to pull him away. Jim had mere seconds to live, and Bill acted fast. He twisted the arm, and it popped as he dislocated the patient's shoulder. That sort of pain should have stopped the patient in his tracks. But it didn't.

Inez ran to Jim with towels, hoping to staunch the flow of blood.

Grace scrambled onto the bed. She balled her hands up into fists and extended the knuckles of her middle fingers. She applied fast, heavy pressure to either side of the jaw. But the patient's jaw remained shut. She held his nose, but that did nothing. She had a hard time maintaining her grip. Every surface was slippery with Jim's blood.

Inez gave a muffled scream. The patient ripped the flesh from Jim's neck. Jim was unconscious from loss of blood. His upper body slumped on the bed. Inez pressed the white towels against his neck. He already appeared drained of blood.

The patient gulped down the lump of Jim's flesh. Then he lunged for Inez. The nurse slammed the bloody towels into the patient's face and threw all her weight against him.

Grace felt the patient's body throw her backward. Bill scooped her off the bed from behind before she lost her balance. "Thanks," she said. The words were barely out of her mouth when the patient turned toward her and tried to bite her. She dodged him as he thrashed at the sheets that covered his legs. She and Bill scooted around to the foot of the bed, out of range of the patient's mouth.

Inez walked backward toward them. "Look! It's *Jim*!"

Grace looked at Jim's white face and his damaged neck. He had already bled out. No one could survive that kind of wound. Yet Jim walked toward Inez. Grace felt her blood run cold. "*Run!*" she yelled. "Get out of the room!"

Inez turned and ran. Grace met her at the door. Bill seemed frozen in position.

"*Jim!*" Bill yelled. "Jim, can you hear me?"

The patient was tangled in his bedclothes, but he was moving toward Bill and clamping his teeth together with a loud chomping noise.

Jim moved toward Bill with his mouth open. A guttural moan escaped from his throat.

Grace pulled open the door and yelled, "Bill, *move!*"

Inez was at Bill's side in a flash. She grabbed Bill's hand and bent his wrist back just enough for the pain to bring him to his senses. Then she pushed him toward the door. The patient freed himself from the bedclothes, and Jim was almost upon them.

Grace, Inez, and Bill ran through the door and closed it. The door latch clicked shut a second before the patient and Jim reached the door.

Michael K. Clancy

Out of Time

Day Two
Georgetown University Medical Center
Washington, D.C.

"BEN, I've got bad news. The Surgeon General is saying your uncle's confession is a hoax. I was told I should tell you nothing. Just that we canceled your slot."

"Tim, you know me. This is no hoax. You're an executive producer. Can't you do something?"

"It's coming from the very top. If I fight them on this, they'll fire me and frog-march me out of here. I'm taking a risk talking to you." Tim paused. "I don't regret it; I'm just telling you how it is."

Dr. Benjamin Lieber's heart sank. The cover-up had started already. Much faster than he expected. "Did the Surgeon General give you talking points?"

"Ben, he's saying the Z-Factor virus is like the flu. He's saying they have it under control. He's saying there's a *cure*."

"He's lying."

"I know."

"Can you get me another time slot on CNN?"

"No. Not yet anyway. You're blacklisted here. The word is out on ABC, CBS, NBC, cable, and everywhere. Even PBS. But it's all over the web. *The New York Times* even posted a blurb online. Ten minutes later, it disappeared."

"Thanks for letting me know."

"You know me too. We've got to do the right thing."

"Yes."

Ben, reports are flooding in. Stuff we aren't allowed to report." Tim sounded worried.

"Tell me."

"Drug deal gone bad. Victim shot in the chest. Victim got up and bit the shooter. Shooter and his pals used all their ammo, and the victim kept coming until he was capped in the head. One of the gang caught it on video and posted it online."

"That must have gotten some attention."

"Not much. News outlets discredited it as a hoax. Poor camera work. Gang related. And murderers don't have a lot of credibility. They played it for laughs. A zombie parody."

"Any credible reports?"

"Hospitals and hospices. The staff is credible, but they didn't catch anything on tape. A couple of hospices reported deaths followed by reanimation and attacks on residents. A hospice in Pennsylvania reported that all its employees fled."

"All of them?"

"Yes. After two were eaten alive."

"Why isn't the local press reporting these incidents? What about international newswires?"

"Suppressed. All of it. The government's PR machine has bombarded the press. The official story is the Surgeon General's story, and it's the story the public wants to believe."

"I get it. If I didn't know better, I'd want to believe it too," said Ben.

"The Surgeon General will be on all the major networks and all the cable programs tonight. That will be followed by segments on how to treat the Z-Factor flu. Stay home from work, fluids, and the usual."

"Tim. Listen to me. They are doing all the wrong things. Within the week, the President will have to declare a state of emergency and martial law. He won't have a choice."

"Do you have numbers?"

"Anyone who claims to know the numbers is a liar. I can only give you estimates based on scenarios."

"Okay."

"In my best-case scenario, everyone is informed, we declare a state of emergency, we track the disease spread, initiate outbreak protocols, and dispatch trained locally-based emergency workers with a legitimate way to guarantee their health and safety."

"How bad?"

"Yesterday was day one. In the best-case scenario, absent Z-Factor, around 6,775 people died in the USA yesterday, mostly in hospitals and hospices, as you already know from your incoming reports. If all those institutions were informed about this and trained for it, they would have a chance to contain it. It wouldn't be easy, and they'd need backup for inevitable crises. And that is the ideal scenario; we're far from that. But people die of a lot of other causes. Outside institutions, it will be even harder to contain this."

"But people would fight back," said Tim.

"Yes. If they realize what they're up against. But they need warning and weapons, and even then, there will be accidents and unavoidable casualties. Staying with this scenario and assuming people fought back so that zombies, on average, each infected only one human, there were 13,550 zombies in the USA this morning. If there are 6,775 usual deaths today, and each of yesterday's zombies, on average, infects one human today, there will be 20,325 zombies by the end of today. That does not count the victims of the people who died today. By the end of tomorrow, day 3, there will be at least 47,000. By the end of day four, the day after tomorrow, there will be over 101,000. Skip ahead to day 13. By then, we're at 50 million in the U.S. alone. One out of every six will be a zombie."

Tim was silent.

"Tim. Are you there?"

"Fifty million?"

"Yes."

"That's your *best-case* scenario?"

"Best case if we do not proactively inform people. If we could immediately inform everyone all at once..."

"An impossible task. We can't reach everyone," said Tim.

"But with news media, we can reach most of them. And if they are ready, willing, and able to take effective action, we can control the numbers before the infection overtakes us."

"But we're not warning people."

"That's my point," said Ben. "It's crucial that we inform everyone right now. Instead, the Surgeon General plans to lie to them."

"So, what does your analysis say about that?"

"It is the end of civilization as we know it. The best we can hope for is defended communities while we do our best to end the swelling number of zombies. If we can hold out, the number of zombies will peak, and we can cull the numbers. Maybe we can find a cure. That is, if thirst, hunger, exposure, other diseases, and other humans don't kill us off."

"I'll see what I can do," said Tim. "But I can't promise anything. I won't get any help from my bosses."

"In a few days, you'll have bigger things to worry about than getting fired."

Out of time. That's the phrase that kept running through Ben's head. He needed an ally. A natural leader. Someone who knew when the existing hierarchy mattered and when it didn't. Someone bold, willing to do what was necessary. Someone who could think on his feet and make quick decisions. Someone who had medical knowledge and who knew how the military and Washington worked and how they didn't work. Ben picked up his phone and called Jack Crown.

Zombie Apocalypse: The Origin

OODA Loop

Day Two
VA Medical Center Washington, D.C.

"THANK YOU for coming, Dr. Crown."

Jack grinned and nuzzled her neck, "It's Jack, *Dr. Grace Waters*. You can save Dr. Crown for after the wedding."

"Not here. I work here."

Jack grew serious and gave a slight nod. It was one of the things he loved about her. Right time. Right place. Don't mix things up. He glanced down the hall. The only other people in the hallway were a man and a woman in white hospital uniforms standing in front of a door at the far end. Usually, the hallways were teeming with life.

"Where is everyone?" he asked.

"Behind closed doors."

Jack shot her a look. "Where's hospital security?"

"I sent them to the intensive care unit. We have a patient who may expire soon."

Jack Crown bent over slightly to better take her in. At five feet seven inches, she was not a short woman, but his six-foot-four-inch frame towered over her. Her long reddish-brown hair was twisted into a low disheveled bun. Her clothes were covered by a hospital gown, an odd look. Her face was pale. The usual softness was gone. And there was something else. An expression he had never seen on her face before. She looked *frightened*.

He had a thousand questions. "You said to come as fast as possible. Is it Legionnaires?"

She shook her head. Then she paused, took a deep breath, and exhaled as if she were trying to calm herself down. "You are going to want to see this." She whirled and started down the empty corridor at a fast walk.

He was at her side in two strides. Jack had never seen her at work before. She wore sensible rubber-soled shoes. None of the silly heels some female doctors wore.

His military-issued phone gave off a loud ring that seemed to echo off the walls. He glanced at the caller's signature, *Dr. Benjamin Lieber*.

"Colonel Crown," he answered.

"Jack, it's Ben. Stop what you're doing and read the executive summary of the email I sent you."

"Ben..."

"Jack, it's urgent."

"Ben, I'm in the middle of something..."

"*Outbreak protocols.*"

"Give me a second," Jack responded into the phone, making sure he was loud enough for Grace to hear. He turned to her. "It's Ben...Dr. Benjamin Lieber at Georgetown. I have to take this."

She stopped and spun around. She stared at him and shifted impatiently. Her blue eyes clouded with worry. She was about to say something, but he raised his left hand, giving her a signal to wait a minute while he accessed his email with his right hand. It took him two minutes to scan the message. He went far beyond the executive summary. If it had come from anyone except Ben, he would have been laughing instead of frowning.

"I have a situation here at the VA medical center," said Jack, "but I'll get there as soon as I can." He finally thought he understood why Grace looked frightened.

"Be careful," said Ben. "If you encounter any, don't let them bite you, scratch you, or, if you can help it, even touch you."

"Got it," said Jack.

"Come on," urged Grace.

"Wait. You'd better read this." He handed her his phone.

She read the summary, and her face took on a look of comprehension as if she had just solved a puzzle. But worry and fear still marred her pretty face. "It's incredible, but it adds up."

He threw her a questioning glance.

"Come on. I'll show you." Her hand trembled as she handed him the phone. Then she spun around and matched his pace as they sped down the corridor.

As they approached the doorway, Jack appraised the brown-haired Caucasian male and a five-foot-five Hispanic woman staring through the square glass window in the door. They appeared horror-stricken. Tears streamed down the man's face.

"Bill and Inez, this is Dr. Crown," Grace said. "Colonel Jack Crown, M.D."

Inez and Bill immediately gave him their full attention. The relief on their faces was obvious. Bill wiped his face, swallowed hard, and seemed to draw on a reserve of courage. They both looked as if they wanted to say something, but Jack just nodded in their direction and stepped forward. They made room so he could look through the glass window.

Jack saw what until now he still had only half believed was possible. Two male zombies pushed against the door. Behind them, the room was covered in old, darkened brownish blood. The bed was at an angle, and medical equipment littered the floor.

One zombie wore a torn, blood-soaked hospital gown, crazily askew. An arm dangled uselessly at his side, and he pushed against the door with his other hand. Before he died, he would have been in his early twenties. Jack was surprised to see such a young man, or what used to be a man. It looked feral, with dull, lifeless eyes. The zombie's stretched lips bared both teeth and gums. A chunk of flesh hung from its mouth, dripping blood. Jack heard its gnashing teeth clatter against the glass as it pushed at the door.

The other zombie wore a blood-soaked hospital uniform. His face was ghostly white, drained of blood, and the left side of his neck was missing. He looked around thirty. Death would have been very fast. He would have passed out almost immediately from the drop in blood pressure as his blood spurted out of his carotid artery. He would have bled out in under a minute. Jack realized why Grace wore the hospital gown. Jim's ten pints of blood covered everything within spurting distance.

"Are there more?" asked Jack.

"One in the morgue. Locked in. Stroke patient died and reanimated on the slab." said Grace.

Jack nodded. That made sense.

"It all happened so fast, in the space of an hour. This incident, and the morgue death," she said. "We had no warning. We're not prepared."

He texted his team for backup, then he asked, "What happened here?"

Grace began, "Young male in his twenties overdosed. We thought he was stabilized, but his heart couldn't take the strain. He coded about an hour and a half ago. We worked on him for forty-five minutes and got his heart back a couple of times, but he kept failing. Finally, I had to pronounce him. Bill is an intern, and Inez is a nurse." She nodded in the direction of the glass square in the door. "Jim was an intern, too. We were all still in the room."

"He was my best friend," Bill said, his voice cracking.

"Jim thought he saw the patient move, and when he leaned over to examine him, the patient bit into his neck," Grace said. "Bill tried to pull the patient off Jim, but…"

"I couldn't get him off Jim," groaned Bill. "I dislocated its shoulder, but the zombie wouldn't stop."

"The masseter is the strongest muscle in the human body," said Jack. Once his jaw clamped down, you had little chance. These things don't feel pain. You're lucky you didn't get bitten yourself."

"I know that now, agreed Bill. The situation was sudden chaos. Fortunately, Dr. Waters' OODA loop reset faster than mine. She and Inez forced me out of the room. They don't seem to know how to open the door. But it is a lever handle, and now and then, they lean on it, and the door swings out a little. There's no lock. So far, we've been able to push them back."

"OODA loop?" asked Grace.

"Later," was all the answer Jack gave her and turned back to Bill. "Military?"

"Civilian...vet." Bill straightened up. "*Veteran*, sir. Iraq." He saluted Jack. "I've heard of you, sir. *Death by Ghost*. It's an honor to meet you."

Out of the corner of his eye, Jack saw another question in Grace's eyes, but that one would have to wait, too. "It's an honor to meet you too. Thank you for your service." He extended his hand, and Bill took it in a firm shake.

"Jim, too," Bill said. He glanced at the window. "We served together. Went to medical school together." Bill's head snapped back to look at Jack. "We always had each other's back. Until now."

"You couldn't have done more under the circumstances; you did your best." Jack knew from experience that was what Bill needed to hear. He'd replay this scene in his mind for a long time to come, and it wouldn't help him to wonder if he could have prevented this tragedy.

"I served in Iraq, too," said Inez. "How do you think I was able to help extricate this bruiser?" She gave Bill a sidelong glance.

"Well done." Jack shook her hand and reminded himself not to make assumptions. "You probably saved his life." Jack looked at the zombies. "It's Z-Factor. If you get bitten or scratched, you'll get infected and die soon after that. Then you will reanimate as one of them. There's no cure. Yet."

Bill paled. "Thanks for pushing me out of there, nurse."

"Inez. Glad I could help." She looked at the former intern with his bared teeth pressed at the window and shuddered. "So, this is Z-Factor. God help us." Her dark brown eyes were deep pools of fear.

Jack saw the door swinging outward a half inch. He pushed back hard and managed to shut it again, but the zombie in the hospital gown was leaning on the lever, and the latch wouldn't catch.

"Hold the door," said Jack. There was no time to wait for backup. These people were exhausted. He couldn't risk the zombies getting out and causing more casualties.

Bill, Inez, and Grace pressed their combined weight against it.

"Bill, I'm sorry about your friend Jim. We're not taking any chances. I'm going to have to put them both down. I'll need everyone's help," said Jack.

"That's not Jim, sir. Not anymore. That thing is the enemy that killed Jim," said Bill. "Tell me what you need."

Jack nodded. Bill's OODA loop was back on track. "Bill, take position next to me."

"Yes, sir." Bill moved next to Jack, away from the door hinge to the crack where it would open, and leaned his weight against it. The women repositioned to accommodate him.

Jack continued, "On the count of three, ease up on the door—enough to let it jerk open around twelve inches or so. Then slam it back hard on my command."

Jack drew his Beretta M-9 service pistol. It was a lousy tactical weapon for most men, but Jack easily disengaged the safety with one hand. Years of practice made the long trigger pull on the first round second nature. He hated using a pistol in close quarters. Lots could go wrong, but it was his best option.

"Bill, as soon as we help slam the door, get into position behind me," Jack said. Then he addressed the women. "As soon as Bill is in position, I'll give the command to fully open the door, fast and wide. I'll lead in with Bill behind me."

"I'll keep the other one away from you while you take out the first one," said Bill.

"Right. Then, step out of the way so I can get a clean shot of the second one. Dr. Waters and Inez, you hang back while we finish them off. Four people will be no good in close quarters. If anything goes wrong, try to close the door and run for it. Backup is coming."

"Got it," said Inez, as Grace and Bill nodded in unison.

Jack saw their look of determination. He knew that these weren't the kind of people who would make a run for it, not if there was a chance of saving someone else. Jack got into position so that when the door swung open, he could step into the gap. "One, two, *three*."

Bill, Grace, and Inez relaxed pressure, and the zombies fell forward toward the opening door.

"Okay, *slam it!*"

Bill, Inez, and Grace shoved hard with Jack's powerful helping hand above their heads. The zombies were thrown off balance, stumbling backward.

Jack and Bill were in position in a flash. "O*pen!*"

Grace and Inez yanked open the door. Jack aimed and shot the hospital-gowned zombie between the eyes. The pistol's sharp report seemed to energize the other one, and it started toward Jack—faster than he expected. Bill moved between Jack and the zombie. Bill dodged its bite, but he didn't have much room to maneuver. Bill pushed back on the zombie's torso, but without leverage, he only managed to knock it back a few inches. It craned its neck toward Bill.

Jack aimed, but Bill was in the way of a clean shot. "Drop!" shouted Jack.

Bill dropped to the floor, and as the zombie bent over to attack him, Jack shot it through the top of its head.

Jack extended his hand and helped Bill to his feet. "Glad you're a vet. Good reaction time. It saved your life."

"Thanks," Bill said with a rueful smile. "It almost had me." He bent down and rested his hand on the corpse's forehead. "I'm sorry, Jim. You deserved better. Rest in peace."

STALE brown blood covered the floor, and the corpses were smeared with it. The room looked like a bulldozer had plowed through it, with soiled equipment and gauze scattered everywhere. The bloody bed stood at an angle from the wall covered with tubes, the IV bottle, and the toppled metal IV stand.

Inez covered the corpses with fresh sheets. They were white mounds in a sea of red and waste.

"I'm taking one to Dr. Benjamin Lieber," Jack said. "He'll want to do an autopsy."

"Alright," said Grace, "you can have them both if you want."

"One will do."

"I have a couple of questions."

"Yes?"

"OODA loop?"

"It's how you deal with uncertainty. Observe, orient, decide, act," replied Jack.

"I'm not sure why Bill would say my OODA loop reset faster than his," said Grace.

"I heard that," said Bill. "You're a fighter. You run toward people who need help, not away from them. Not if you don't have to. You climbed up on that bed and tried to get that thing off Jim when you still thought it was human. Even I didn't do that. But somehow, you realized conditions had changed. You were the first one to get it. You were the one who told us to run."

Jack nodded. "Sounds like your OODA loop is doing just fine."

"Okay," said Grace. "One more. Death by Ghost?"

Jack said nothing.

"Jack?"

He noticed she didn't say Dr. Crown or even Colonel Crown. Conditions at work had changed. The old hierarchies didn't matter as much. But he didn't answer her question. "Some other time. I must get back to Ben. I'll leave two of my men here at the hospital to back up your security. They are bringing arms."

"I see them now," said Grace.

Four soldiers with assault rifles and side arms strode down the hall and were soon upon them. The major spoke for his men. "Major Juan Chavez reporting for duty. We read Dr. Lieber's message."

"Yes. It's real," said Jack. "Stay here with one of your men. I'll take a corpse and two men with me."

The soldiers investigated the open doorway. One let out a low whistle.

"Looks as if you started the party without us, colonel," said Chavez.

"There's one in the morgue. I want each of you to look for himself before I clear out of here. Take it out. Headshot. ICU already has eyes. Security is handling it, so you're just backup," said Jack, "so let them know how to reach you. Follow outbreak protocols until Dr. Lieber and I can craft zombie protocols."

"Yes, sir," said Chavez. "We'll track any incoming bites or other Z-Factor casualties."

"I know this doesn't need saying, but don't take any unnecessary risks," said Jack.

Chavez gave a slight nod.

"Have you notified your families?" asked Jack.

"Yes," said Chavez. "Two of my men will relieve me in four hours; they're with their families now. Then, we'll check on our families and make sure they are following protocols. Sometimes, they must hear it directly from you. We'll have emailed pictures to everyone by then to drive the point home."

"Chavez, can you post them online?"

"Yes, sir."

"Use all of the military boards you have access to. Tell your kids to spread the word to all of their friends and social media, too," said Jack.

"Inez, Chavez will supply photos and anything else we have. Can you post this information on nurses' forums?"

"Yes, Dr. Crown. Right away," said Inez.

"Sir, where is everyone?" asked Chavez. Unease crept into his voice. "Are they all right?"

"They're alive," said Jack. He gestured to the doors. "They're in the rooms. You might get them to start spreading the word that it's safe to come out."

"Sir?"

"Yes?"

"What if people want to leave for home?" asked Chavez.

"You mean staff?"

"Staff and patients."

"Let them," said Jack. "Unless they are scratched or bitten."

"Sir?"

"What?"

"It's not outbreak protocol…"

"Right, but they are not contagious unless they are scratched, bitten, or dead. And if they are dead, I know you will deliver the headshot long before a zombie tries to walk out of here. Just so you have cover, that's an order, major."

Chavez smiled.

"Why are you smiling?"

"Sir, you just gave the first of the new zombie protocols."

Yes, I guess I have, Jack thought. "Let me clarify. We've never seen anything like this. We can't force people to separate themselves from their families. They have the right to protect their loved ones. You'll have to make do with people who are willing to stay. Only the infected will be required to stay. They need to be isolated. See that they are cared for. If they become gravely ill, restrain them. If they die, end them with a headshot."

"Yes, sir," said Chavez, visibly relieved.

Jack and Bill looked for a gurney while the soldiers went to the morgue to kill their first zombie.

Within ten minutes, they had the body strapped to a gurney and loaded into an ambulance. Jack found Grace in the middle of her rounds.

"Come with me?"

"I'm needed here," said Grace. "Two doctors left before you arrived. I sent Inez and Bill home. They need to warn their families and make their own decisions."

"I'm coming back for you," said Jack.

"Find me at my place. Tonight. I need to clean up."

Chavez knocked on the door. "Sir, the men are ready to accompany you to Georgetown Medical Center."

"Sitrep."

"All clear. Zombie in the morgue was dispatched with one shot."

"Good work," said Jack with a slight nod. "Take care of Dr. Waters for me." Then Jack strode out the door.

"DEATH by Ghost," said Grace after she finished her rounds on the top floor and strode with Chavez toward the elevator bank. "Can you tell me what that means?"

"He never told you? You're getting married in two weeks."

"It's just the way he is. He'll answer any direct question, but you must know what to ask. He doesn't volunteer a lot."

"But..."

"It's not a trick question, Major Chavez. I'm asking because I don't know."

"Of course. Sorry, Dr. Waters. He got that nickname in Iraq when he was a sniper."

"I knew he was a sniper, a field doctor. One of the few soldier doctors."

"Yes, ma'am. I mean, Dr. Waters."

"So, why the nickname?"

"He took a Daesh commander's head clean off. It was right in the middle of a lesson for recruits on how to behead captives."

"So why not Death by Sniper?" asked Grace.

"Thing is, he was about a mile away. He's that good."

Grace couldn't hide the pride in her voice. "He gave those recruits the surprise of their lives."

"There's a British guy, Corporal Craig Harrison. He did it first, from over 8,000 feet. He holds the record. But Colonel Crown got the nickname. Come to think of it, he probably didn't tell you because he didn't want to steal Corporal Harrison's thunder. As you said, it's the way he is."

Grace said nothing.

"Do you mind if I ask a personal question?" asked Chavez.

"Shoot."

"Does it bother you?"

"What?" asked Grace.

"That he doesn't volunteer stuff."

"No." Grace shrugged. "I don't like to bring work home with me, either."

"You're a good match," grinned Chavez.

Grace was silent for a moment. "Death by Ghost. I like it."

"I do, too," Chavez agreed. "I'd follow him into hell."

"I would too, but it's not the kind of thing you say to a guy right before you get married."

Chavez laughed.

Grace clenched his arm. "Did you hear that?" she said in a low voice.

As the elevator neared the ground floor, the screams grew louder.

"Get back," said Chavez, readying his assault rifle.

When the doors opened, the hallway was empty. The screams came from around the corner, the hallway to the Emergency Department. Chavez pulled out his radio.

"*Wait*," whispered Grace. "Sound attracts them."

Preparations

Day Two
Georgetown University Medical Center
Washington, D.C.

"THE CORPSE is in the cooler, Ben," said Jack Crown. He had already briefed Ben on the events at the Veteran's Medical Center earlier that day. "But there isn't time for an autopsy. We'll have to bring it with us. I've sent more men to the outbreak compound to secure it and add more supplies. Their plane is on its way to Virginia. We'll recheck the infrastructure and systems and secure the area."

Jack and Ben stood face to face. At six feet three inches, Ben was an inch shorter than Jack, and he was fit in the way a conscientious gym rat is fit. Jack's body was a mass of hardened trained muscle, a tightly coiled spring of potential energy.

Ben nodded in agreement. "No one has been warned. As you predicted, in the worst-case scenario, Washington is lying while apparatchiks gather resources to save themselves at the expense of everyone else.

We've never seen anything like Z-Factor before. Tell your men their families need to prepare today for evacuation early tomorrow. Those who are ready can go now. Transports are ready. We'll conduct our research at the outbreak compound."

"We're moving sooner than any of our drills predicted, but I don't see an alternative," said Jack.

"Zombie protocols." Ben massaged his brow. "Let's keep up the momentum so our people get to the compound and try one more time to get the media to warn people."

This was worse than their most extreme scenario. A fast-moving virus, worse than the Black Plague. They had to hunker down and wait out the epidemic. But there was a difference. Everyone was infected, and every death created a fresh zombie. It was an evergreen disease. If they didn't move out before panic set in, they'd never get out of D.C.

Ben said, "While you were busy at the Veteran's Medical Center, I had the onsite skeleton crew at the outbreak compound give me a preliminary report. We have fuel stores on site for 18 months. Our offsite dedicated refinery and our offsite oil reserves have security in place. Electricity and backup generators are operational. We have blackout mechanisms to avoid attracting scavengers. Water systems and chlorine are in great shape. Human waste disposal systems are set. Our farmland and fertilizer are in great shape. For the past two years, we've been selling the food, but it will be enough to sustain us indefinitely, provided we can keep it secure. We've moved vehicles into the garages and more parts and supplies into the mechanical shop. Medicine and supplies are in place."

"How many are coming in?" asked Jack.

"As you know, capacity is 155. We have 92 people coming in. Maybe 95," said Ben. "Why? Are you adding someone?"

"Grace," replied Jack. "You know we're not married yet. We said wives and kids only."

"I know. We were wrong."

Jack said nothing.

Ben smiled for the first time that day. "I already have her on the list. Three more fiancés, too. Proviso is they must marry at the Compound. The chaplain will do it free of charge; it's one of the perks you military guys have. That should have been our protocol all along. I'm changing things as we go."

"Yes. About our forecasts…"

"Here," said Ben, handing him the numbers.

"We're too low."

"What do you mean?"

"Today. At the V.A. Center. The second intern, a vet no less, told me he froze when he was in mortal danger."

"What do you mean he froze?"

"His OODA loop didn't reset fast enough," explained Jack. He didn't know what he was observing. He couldn't orient himself to the new reality. He faced his dead, reanimated friend, but he couldn't take in what had just happened. He couldn't make a decision, much less take appropriate action."

"But he wasn't bitten."

"It was a near thing. Grace gave the order to run. The nurse snapped to it and helped get him away."

"Grace gave the order?"

"Yes. She has more experience. She knew the man was dead, yet he was walking, and he was a threat. She processed it fast, even though she didn't exactly know what she was dealing with."

"We have to alert first responders," said Ben.

"Yes, but there's more."

"More?"

"Yes. When I arrived, Grace didn't spring the news on me. She knew I had to see it for myself. Even after you called me, I still didn't completely believe it. Not until I saw them myself."

"I get it," said Ben. "We need to capture something on film and release it through credible channels."

"Cameraman's on his way."

"I already spoke to General Markum. He's arranged a meeting at the White House per outbreak protocols."

The White House

Day Two
Washington, D.C.

THEY sailed through White House security and were immediately ushered into the Oval Office. *At least some of our outbreak protocols are working*, thought Jack.

General Markum, the Surgeon General, the Secretary of Homeland Security, POTUS, the Vice President, the Senate minority and majority leaders, the Speaker of the House, and the House minority leader were already in the room.

Jack groaned inwardly. *Politicians.* He already knew this wasn't going to end well. "Are we waiting for the Secretary of Defense?"

General Markum and POTUS exchanged a glance.

"He's already moved to a remote location," replied General Markum.

It was Jack and Ben's turn to exchange a look.

You mean he's already on the run to save his own hide, thought Jack. They expected this.

In a super virus crisis, so-called leaders would hoard the facts, abandon ship, and keep the public in the dark.

"We need to discuss what to tell the public," said the Homeland Security Secretary.

General Markum glanced at Ben, who gave him a slight nod. "*Everything*," said General Markum.

Jack was grateful for Ben's foresight. He had crafted vital clauses in the Outbreak Emergency Bill, passed by Congress and signed into law by this President two years ago.

The Secretary of Homeland Security protested, "That isn't your decision, it's..."

"The White House makes that decision," interrupted the Senate Majority Leader.

General Markum interrupted right back. "You should read the Bills you pass."

"What is the location of the Outbreak Compound, and where is the airstrip for the evacuation planes?" asked the Head of Homeland Security.

"You know we can't tell you that," replied General Markum.

"It has an underground bunker to withstand a nuclear blast?" asked the Senate Majority Leader.

General Markum said nothing.

That was fast, thought Jack. *The news reports must be bad.* The team knew that Washington's elite would make a grab for resources to save themselves and abandon the people they were supposed to represent, but they didn't expect it on the first day. But then, the world had changed overnight. These were zombie protocols.

"Never mind," the Senate Majority Leader said. "I've seen the specs. I know it does. Impressive. Now, where is it?"

"I can't tell you that either," said General Markum.

"*I'm* asking," said the President.

"Not even you, sir," said General Markum. "Your emergency command compound is secure, and you know where that is. You'll be well taken care of. But I cannot reveal the location of our research compound."

The President glared at Markum. "*I insist*. My friends..."

"As we explained when the Outbreak Bill was crafted. The emergency research team has to put the oxygen mask over its own face first, or it won't be able to get the job done to help anyone else," said General Markum.

"I'm overriding that. Here's the Executive Order." POTUS handed General Markum a sheet of paper.

Jack saw the Congressmen shift in their seats and lean forward. They seemed to be enjoying themselves.

"Dr. Benjamin Lieber," said General Markum without glancing at the document. "I'd like you to weigh in."

Ben stood up, knowing his height was an advantage. "I will not comply until I finish challenging this in court."

"But that will take…" The President's eyes widened as reality sunk in.

Ben had been given legal authority over Outbreak Protocols: secrecy and clearance, resources for his team—everything. Full discretionary powers. Ben wasn't military; he wasn't in the normal chain of command. They could still fight him for control of the media, but they couldn't force Ben to expose his team.

General Markum and Jack rose to their feet and stood at Ben's side.

"We'll say goodbye now," said Ben. "We have work to do."

BEN waited as Jack and General Markum retrieved their side arms at the White House exit. He saw them both tense as two Secret Service agents walked briskly toward them.

One of the agents called out to General Markum, "Sir, please hold up a minute."

"What is it?" boomed General Markum.

At the sound of General Markum's voice, the Secret Service agents stepped back a pace despite themselves. "Sir, we're asking for a professional courtesy."

"Yes?"

The agents looked at each other and then back at the general. "Z-Factor, sir. We're hearing..." The agent paused. "I feel silly for even asking about it..."

"Out with it," said the general impatiently.

"Zombies. We heard Z-Factor turns you into a zombie."

"You heard correctly. But only if you die, get bitten, or get scratched. Try to avoid those things if you can. We're trying to find a cure." With that, the general turned to Ben and Jack and said, "*Let's go!*"

Just before he turned to leave, Ben caught sight of the agents staring open-mouthed at the general. He could feel their eyes on their backs as they walked away.

"TELL your men to call their families. Evacuate everyone who isn't absolutely needed here right now. We'll follow tomorrow morning," said Ben. Then he called his wife. "Julia?"

"Hi honey, I picked up Carl. We locked up and set the alarm," she said. "Dinner's almost ready. When will you be home?"

"I'm not coming home. I need you to evacuate. Right now. I'll join you tomorrow."

"*Now*? This isn't how the protocols are supposed to work. I don't want to leave without you."

"New data. New protocols. Zombie protocols. You can't wait for me. I'll get out tomorrow. I've got protection, but I can't spare men to fetch you. I can't worry about you and Carl and do my job. Don't forget your carry permit and your gun. If you wait until tomorrow, you may not make it out. Go right now and call me when you're on the plane, and call me when you get there."

"It's that bad?"

"Worse. Politicos will try to seize transports, and we don't want to jam everyone in at the last minute. Get out while you can."

"Okay, but you're sure you'll get out? The Outbreak Compound needs you more than they need me. I'd feel better if I had eyes on you."

"Positive. I'm with General Markum and Jack Crown."

"Okay," said Julia, "You're in good hands. Those two could get you out of Sing Sing. What about the car?"

"Park it at the airstrip with the keys in the ignition in case someone needs to move it. It's going to get hectic."

"Got it. We're leaving right now. Love you."

"Love you too."

Ben was relieved. When Julia said she was going to do something, it got done. "General Markum," Ben said, "Is your family underway?"

"Yes," he said. "The speed of events has my wife a little off balance, but she's not a complainer. With any luck, Barbara and Julia will share the same transport."

"What about you, Jack?" asked Ben. The moment he looked at Jack's face, he knew something was wrong.

"I called Grace. She texted back: 'E.R. Zombies. Twenty or more. Send help.'"

"Then go," said Ben.

Jack nodded. "I already texted my team. It's only around four miles; I'll take a taxi. A dozen men will meet me there. We should arrive at about the same time. And I asked the cameraman to meet us. We might get some useful footage."

Michael K. Clancy

Evacuation

Day Two
VA Medical Center Washington, D.C.

CHAVEZ took out a tactical mirror and looked back around the corner. He offered Grace a quick look. Zombies crowded the small emergency reception area, eating five or six people alive. It was a bloodbath.

So far, the zombies hadn't noticed them, and they weren't on the move. He signaled for Grace to move backward down the empty hall to the elevators. As soon as she was on the move, he walked quickly backward, glancing over his shoulder to be sure it remained clear.

Grace felt her mobile vibrate. *Jack.* She texted him, and then she tapped Chavez on the shoulder and showed him her message to Jack. Then she typed, *Set phone to vibrate.*

Chavez motioned that his radio was already off, and his mobile was set to vibrate. He indicated she should keep moving. He pulled out his phone and texted the soldier he had sent to the critical care unit. *Zombies in E.R. Warn people. Meet on second floor. Silent.*

They got in the elevator and rode to the second floor.

Grace looked at her phone. "Ben gave the evacuation order."

Captain Shiller arrived with two security guards. They were just in time to hear Grace report the news. "Ready to move, sir."

Chavez put Captain Shiller and the guards in the picture and then asked Grace, "How big is this place?"

"We have 175 acute care beds, 90% filled. Thirty beds in the psych ward. Twenty suites in another ward. There are 120 beds in the adjacent Community Living Center. Mostly hospice and geriatric long-term care."

"Those zombies in the Emergency Department. They looked old to me. The fresh victims looked a lot younger."

"I was thinking the same thing," said Grace.

"What do you think happened?"

"Just a guess. Someone must have died in the Community Living Center. With no warning, they were sitting ducks. Then, the zombies went looking for more food. People seeking emergency care looked like dinner."

Chavez called Jack. "We're on the second floor of the Medical Center. There may be more than 120 hostiles on the ground. At least twenty inside the building in the Emergency Department. They may have moved, and there may be more already inside. We do not have eyes on the ground."

"I'm outside," said Jack. "I was in a taxi and had to get out. The team picked me up about a mile away. Zombies fanned out in a one-block radius around the Center. We cleared a path in. We will probably have to clear the path again on the way out. We can clear out the ER. Meet us on the ground floor. Take the stairs in case something goes wrong with the elevators. Move fast. The National Guard is on its way, and after that, it will be a bigger mess."

"On our way," said Chavez.

"May I have a weapon?" asked Grace.

"Do you know how to use this?" Chavez handed her a Remington 1911.

She nodded. "Jack taught me."

"Let's go," said Chavez and headed toward the stairs.

¤

"UPLOAD that film footage to this website and email the file to Dr. Lieber," Jack told the cameraman.

"Already done," said the cameraman.

"Good. Zoom in on that doorway below. The one with the horde. We'll show them how it's done."

Jack and his men were in position on the second floor of the building across from the emergency center. They positioned their rifles and started picking off the zombies in the emergency center. The noise from the falling zombies seemed to draw them together, making the task easier. But it drew a few from the street, so they cleared a path from their building to the Medical Center. Then they scrambled down the stairs and ran through the street and the doors of the Emergency Department, handguns at the ready. They shot two zombies in the hallway.

Grace, Chavez, and Shiller were already down the stairs and met them halfway through the hallway with the two security guards in tow. People peered out of the doorways, and Jack yelled that the National Guard was on its way. The two security guards accompanied them back through the Emergency Department. After Grace, Chavez, and Shiller exited the building, the guards secured the doors.

"Will the National Guard be able to handle this?" asked Grace.

Jack said nothing. He felt his phone's vibration and answered. "Hi, Ben. We just left the VA Medical Center. Zombies are roaming the streets. My men brought four Humvees. We're going to barrel our way out of this zone."

"Take no chances," said Ben. "Do whatever is necessary. No point staying until morning. Head out to the airstrip as soon as you can."

"Will do. Did you get the footage?"

"Yes. A nurses' website picked it up, and it's gone viral. All the internet news sites posted it, and CNN is airing it within the hour. They can try to deny the facts, but people will see the video for themselves and draw their own conclusions. At least now they'll have a chance to fight back."

"Did Julia and Carl leave?"

"They're in the air, along with a lot of team members and their families. I'm glad we moved the schedule ahead."

Jack looked out the window. "Yes, so am I. If I don't see you at the airstrip, I'll see you at the Compound."

Drivers in cars ahead of them saw the Humvees in their rear-view mirrors and pushed through the streets. They ignored the zombies as if they were drunks weaving around them. So far, the zombies didn't block their paths. Instead, they made their way toward the sides of the cars, where they could see people. Meals on wheels.

Within three blocks, they were clear. No zombies in sight. *Ben was right*, Jack thought. If they had waited another day, it would have been much harder to get their team to the airstrip.

Jack and Grace got out at her apartment in Georgetown. "We'll take Grace's car to the airstrip. Keep secure communication lines open, but if I'm a few minutes behind you, don't wait. We'll rendezvous at the Compound. The main thing is to keep everyone moving as fast as they can."

Grace and Jack ran up the stairs.

"Here's a list of things you can bring. One bag," said Jack. "And everything else you will need you can find at the Compound."

"What about you?" asked Grace. One of my men already collected my things from my place. They'll be at the Compound before I will."

"Can you pack for me while I take a shower? You know my place as well as I do. You spend so much time here."

That was true enough. They co-owned the apartment. They purchased it to live in after the wedding. Jack's lease was almost up, and half of his things were already here. "Yes. I'll even put a couple of dinners in the microwave."

"Thanks." Grace kissed him on the mouth and left for the bathroom.

Within an hour, they were finishing their fast food. Jack had forgotten how fragile she looked with her thick reddish-brown hair flowing around her shoulders. Her face was soft and feminine. Her red sweater and black jeans showed off her trim figure. She never wore jewelry to work because she said it got in the way, but he noticed she had put the engagement ring he gave her back on her finger. "Ben says the chaplain can marry us at the Compound. Is that all right with you?"

"The world has changed. Zombie protocols. We're together. That's the main thing."

He smiled. "Right. Let's go."

"Can I take another bag?"

"Grace..."

"My black medical bag. It's fully kitted out."

"Yes," he said instantly. "We can never have enough of those." she retrieved the bag from a small hutch near the door, and he gathered up the trash for the dumpster. As he locked the door, Jack wondered if he'd ever see this place again.

Michael K. Clancy

BOOK 3

ZOMBIE CONTAGION

Anomalies

Day Four
Outbreak Compound, Virginia

BEN, the problem with your numbers is that you forgot that not everyone is like you. You grew up in a stable home with good values. You have a medical degree and a broad education beyond that. The cities are falling faster than we expected. Detroit, St. Louis, Chicago, Oakland, Memphis, Birmingham, Atlanta, Baltimore, Stockton, Cleveland, and Buffalo are struggling already." Jack Crown's large, toned body tensed, and he let out a heavy sigh as they watched the carnage on CNN.

"I thought people would pull together," said Ben.

"Maybe they would have if the government had told them what they were up against right from the start. Some are already pulling together, but I can't stop thinking about Fat Freddy."

"Fat Freddy?"

"Here's a Baltimore cop's hurried email to his dad, a retired cop, two days ago. While we were on the plane on our way here, cops were dealing with the first of the wreckage. Read it and weep."

*****

Dad—Count me out of the softball game tonight. Last night was the busiest night of my career. The shift started with seven fatal shootings in four separate incidents, including a homicide in what was, up until last night, a peaceful black-owned bar near West Mulberry.

At 2:17 a.m., we got a call of a shooting three blocks away in a vacant lot. We pulled up to the place. It was knee-deep in weeds. Fat Freddy, a 300 lb. gas station attendant, was shot multiple times in the torso, chest, and abdomen, an easy big target. I counted nine holes, and he was spraying blood like a lawn sprinkler.

It was 2 a.m., but people came out and screamed at us that he was dying as if we couldn't see that. *Where was the ambulance?* We called to ask for the ETA on the ambulance and called for backup, enough for crowd control.

My partner and I fended off a fast-growing crowd, getting angrier by the second, as Fat Freddy lay bleeding to death on the ground. The mood was beyond ugly. A male voice yelled: *"The cops shot Freddy for no reason."* The crowd was ready to rip us apart. My partner drew his weapon.

Fat Freddy's friends arrived in the nick of time and saved our hash. There were three of the meanest, toughest gangbangers, each with long records. I was never so happy to see three violent, angry black men at night in my life. They flattened the biggest jackass in the crowd and held him on the ground. One of them held the jerk down, and the other two cleared a way in the crowd for the first responders.

Backup never arrived, and there were no more ambulances to be had last night. The city's resources were stretched beyond the limit. Fat Freddy bled out within half an hour. But the crowd wouldn't leave, and they got into a shouting match with Fat Freddy's friends. Next thing you know, Fat Freddy lurched toward us, growling. He raised his lips over his gums and gnashed his exposed teeth. His face was the color of cigarette ash. It's harder to kill a big guy than you might think. Maybe all that fat saved him. Fat Freddy's friends shoved us out of the way to help him.

Fat Freddy bit the biggest guy in the neck, and the victim dropped like a stone. As Fat Freddy chewed a large bloody clump of flesh, he turned toward the screaming crowd. Raw flesh hung from his mouth. He turned toward the victim for another bite. His other friend intervened, and Freddy took a chunk out of his arm. The crowd became a chaotic mob. Gunshots were coming at us from the crowd. A bullet hit Fat Freddy's friend. The one with the arm wound. It grazed his leg. He drew a gun and fired back into the crowd.

My partner and I couldn't believe what we were seeing. Fat Freddy tried to bite his friend in the neck, the one who had just fired his weapon. My partner shot Fat

Freddy again, but we both knew it was useless, and the gunshot enraged the crowd, not to mention Fat Freddy's two remaining friends. The third friend, the one holding the jerk to the ground, let the jerk go and came after my partner. Meanwhile, Fat Freddy's neck-wound friend was dead, and Fat Freddy batted away the one with the arm wound and made a beeline for my partner.

My partner shot him again. My partner and I moved back as Freddy's friends came after us. The one with the bitten arm shot at us without aiming and missed. We returned fire, and he went down. Fat Freddy was on him in a flash and began eating him. His third friend was the only one still standing.

Now we had the crowd at our backs, blocking our exit from the vacant lot with the original jackass somewhere behind us. One or more shooters in the crowd were sending wild bullets our way, but nothing was hitting a target, not that they seemed to be aiming. That got a lot of people running away from the vacant lot.

Fat Freddy and his three friends were still in front of us. Two of Fat Freddy's friends were dead, and the third drew his weapon. He didn't know whether to shoot Fat Freddy, us, or the crowd. He faced the crowd in confusion. I shouted at him to look out. The guy Fat Freddy bit in the neck was up and moving fast in his direction. The third friend spun around and emptied his weapon before his friend fell on him and ripped into his abdomen with his teeth. The guy screamed for us to shoot his friend. We did, but he didn't stop.

My partner and I crouched, and I glanced toward what was left of the crowd. The jackass was shoving a couple of neighbors, trying to clear a path out of the lot. He shouted at people to run, and the crowd ran, but not before firing more bullets our way. My partner was hit in the lower left leg. We had to retreat. I helped him balance on his good leg and hoped that the remnant of the mob standing on the sidewalk at the edge of the vacant lot wouldn't force us to shoot. I thanked God that our car looked like it hadn't been touched. We made it back to the car, and I drove my partner to the emergency room myself. It was a miracle we made it out of the neighborhood alive. I'm beat, but they called me in for a double shift, and I can use the overtime.

Dad—After writing the above, our squad had its morning briefing. You probably already know all about the Z-Factor virus turning people into zombies from your network of retired cops, but the public still doesn't know. The government is still saying everything is under control.

Those of us who worked overtime from the night shift shared our stories. This is a cluster. *Why didn't anyone tell us what Z-Factor really was before this? Why is mainstream media lying to the public about it?*

Looking back, we would have used headshots. Maybe it was better that my partner and I didn't know last night. If we had used headshots and dropped those big men, the crowd probably would have killed us. But as it is, four powerful zombies have probably spawned a zombie jamboree. God help those people. About eighty percent of officers showed up for the day shift. After the briefing, everyone was quiet, but several cops drove home, and nobody thought less of them.

I'm heading home now. Can you meet me there and leave with Claire and the kids? Cops are leaving in droves to get their families out of the city, and some say they'll be back to help. We've been understaffed for years. We don't have the men, training, or equipment to handle this. The National Guard may be able to carve out green zones, but how are they going to get a panicked city under control first? Within a few days, this will likely spin out of control. I'm calling you now to make sure you got this. Let me know if you'll leave the city with us or take your own route. We're heading to the cabin.

*****

"SO, they got out of Dodge," said Ben.

"Not exactly. He got his family to his cabin, and then he and his father returned to Baltimore. Cops and retired cops returned to help."

"Jack, you seem to have a better handle on human nature than I do, but you grew up in a good home, you have a medical degree, and you're a Colonel in the army."

"I wasn't always a colonel. Iraq. I served with all sorts, and we—"

"I get it. I've lived in a rarified environment," Ben agreed.

"But I have no idea how fast this spreads."

"Our initial projections were that 6,775 die every day unrelated to the Z-Factor virus," said Ben. "If each zombie bit on average one person, on average, there would have been 13,550 zombies at the start of the next day. Add to that 6,775 deaths the next day, plus yesterday's. If the new day's zombies each bite one person, there would be 20,325 zombies by the next day's end. By the end of day 7, there would be 840,000 zombies."

"That's about one in every 380 people."

"But if you assume each zombie bites four people," continued Ben, "we're at almost 37 million people by the end of the week."

Jack nodded. "Ten percent of the population. And the day after that, nearly half the population."

It will vary widely by location, how fast people act to kill threats, and how well they pull together to defend themselves. But any area that loses control is a threat to the stability of all the surrounding areas."

A young woman in a lab coat knocked on the open door to get their attention. "Dr. Lieber. Dr. Crown, or do you prefer Colonel?"

"When I'm in the lab, Dr. Crown works for me," replied Jack.

She nodded and handed Ben a sheet of paper. "You asked me to let you know if anyone was bitten but didn't get ill and turn into a zombie."

"What have you found?" asked Ben with a note of hope in his voice.

"Nothing," she said ruefully. "There are no reports of resistance, much less immunity."

"DAD, look what's happening in Chicago." Carl Lieber leaned his six-foot-tall body against the door frame. At seventeen, he wasn't finished growing. He was thin and lanky, as if the calories couldn't keep up with his latest growth spurt. But there was no awkwardness about him. He had his father's good looks and his mother's coloring. His eyes were dark green, and his hair was light brown instead of Ben's dark brown. In every other way, including his piercing intelligence, Carl resembled Ben.

Ben and Jack turned their gaze to the large flat-screen television.

"No, not there, on YouTube." Carl showed them the video playing on his tablet. It was titled Mothers Against Zombies. Six armed black women posed for the camera. Two appeared to be grandmothers. Then, the scene changed to show them covering each other while they killed two zombies. After the segment, one of the women turned to the camera. "You are either with us or against us. We won't tolerate looters, break-ins, or people who won't stand with us."

Ben and Jack exchanged a look.

"It looks as if people are banding together in ways we didn't expect," observed Jack.

"And look at this," said Carl. "People Nation and Folk Nation have banded together to end zombies."

"Who are they?" asked Ben.

"Dad, People Nation includes gangs like the Vice Lords, Black P. Stones, Latin Kings, and some other gangs. Folk Nation includes Gangster Disciples, Black Disciples, Spanish Cobras, and a few other gangs. They figured out fast that when they were fighting each other, the dead rose as zombies. So, they decided they had a much bigger problem than each other. Since the political Ward Captains in the highest crime areas are gang bangers, they called meetings and hammered out a deal."

Carl played another video, and a group of young men showing off weapons said almost the same thing as the Mothers Against Zombies. Except they added: "Stealing food and shooting at the living will get you a bullet in the head. We're giving safe passage to food trucks. Keep distribution lines open."

"They figured that out fast," said Jack. "Drug dealers understand supply lines. I wish them luck."

But there was a lot of bad news from Chicago, too. Some rival gang members were using the mayhem to settle old scores. One group of idiots did drive-by shootings of rival gangs, aiming anywhere but the head.

"Right," said Jack. "It's the same story in almost every city. Some people band together to preserve order. Others work full time to destroy it."

"How will we know when it is safe to go back?" asked Carl. "The news said phone service is breaking down."

Jack dodged the meat of Carl's question. It might never be safe to go back. He replied, "We can transmit and receive radio signals from long distances. We have a signal booster and long-range reception capabilities, even if the people we are talking to do not."

"We'll just have to wait and see, Carl," said Ben. "Meanwhile, we have to do our part."

"Okay," said Carl, "Mom said dinner will be ready at 7:00. Dr. Waters and Dr. Crown are invited too."

DR. GRACE WATERS had showered and changed into black slacks and a deep purple sweater by the time Jack knocked on her door. She fell into his arms and kissed him warmly on the mouth.

"Do you want to be late for dinner?" Jack asked with a grin.

"Yes, but we can't be late. Julia has been working like a demon all day, and she made sure she'd have dinner promptly at seven, so we shouldn't keep her waiting."

Jack almost hid his disappointment, but not quite.

"I'll make it up to you afterward." Grace gave him a seductive smile.

"That's a mood lifter," said Jack. "For a minute, I thought you were going to tell me I was in solitary until the wedding."

"Just two days away," said Grace. "But I won't keep you waiting." Her eyes searched his face. "I know things are a godawful mess, but I'm happy, Jack. I don't think I've ever been happier."

"Me too," Jack assured her. "It looks as if we finally have time to really get to know each other."

"I feel like I know you. I felt that way right away." She moved closer and held him tight. "You don't have to go out of the compound yet, do you?"

"Just outside the gate to dig trenches. For now, anyway. But you know I'll have to go out sometime. Even as well-supplied as we are, there will be things we'll need. There always are."

She swept back her thick reddish-brown hair, and her blue eyes met his. "When you do, I'm going with you. You're more valuable to the team than I am."

"We both know that isn't true."

Grace said nothing.

"Fertile women are more important than men; they're the only ones who can carry the next generation of children if we ever come out of the other side of this apocalypse."

Grace still said nothing. She stepped back and looked at him. Strong, trained, fit, handsome, and crazy smart. A doctor, a colonel. Yet he was telling her that any fertile female was more important. She didn't want to live in this new world if she had to live without him.

He looked at her tenderly. "Promise me..."

"What?"

"Promise me you won't throw yourself on my funeral pyre."

She almost smiled at his choice of words, but she said nothing.

"I mean it, Grace. If anything happens to me, I want you to find someone else. I want you to live. As long as you are alive, a part of me lives with you." Jack's own words surprised him. He never loved anyone as much as he loved Grace, and it wasn't until he said the words that he realized just how much. "But I don't plan on dying. Not anytime soon, anyway."

MORALE at the Compound depended on keeping people productively occupied. Everyone had a job; everyone contributed. They had been at the Compound only two days, but it already felt as if the place was running smoothly on a tight schedule.

"I'm taking charge of inventory for food stores and of the maintenance schedule for plumbing and the gym equipment," said Julia as she served dinner. "We are extremely well stocked. We also seem to have enormous stores of pure honey. Whose idea was that?"

Dr. Grace Waters stirred in her chair at that news. "It keeps forever without spoiling, and it's a natural antiseptic." Her eyes locked on Jack's. The bigger picture of their situation was finally sinking in. She and Jack had talked about honey as one of the items to store in the event of a prolonged disaster. In the worst-case scenario, the U.S. government might be crazy enough to use nuclear weapons. The living would be collateral damage. That's why they had an underground bunker that could withstand a nuclear blast.

Jack saw the alarm in Grace's eyes and changed the topic. "We're bulldozing a wide, deep trench on the outside perimeter of the fence. An electrified fence won't keep zombies out any better than a regular fence, so we don't have to waste electricity."

"Won't the zombies back away from a trench?" asked Julia.

"Apparently not. Their immunity to sensation and pain is a strength, but it is also a weakness. In a way, they are also like lepers. Leprosy causes people to lose sensation, so they don't have a recoil response. That's why lepers lose fingers, toes, and limbs. In the case of zombies, they don't seem to back away from anything hazardous, and they don't try to prevent themselves from falling."

"So it will be like a dry moat," said Julia.

"Yes. The trench will prevent humans in vehicles from ramming the fences, and it can trap zombies if they somehow get past our snipers."

"Dad, can I train with weapons?" asked Carl.

"We're all going to train. Even your mother and Dr. Waters."

Carl couldn't hide his surprise. "I'm glad you're okay with it. But seriously, mom is going to train?"

"The snipers will perform better if we can give them a break, and Jack supplied us with prototype weapons."

"A prototype?" Carl persisted.

Jack explained. "The XR-30 has built-in infrared and suppressor. The scope has a high-grade electronic tracking system. It locks onto your target. The computer does the rest. You can hit a moving target at a range of around 2,000 meters. That's almost one and a quarter miles. You can hit a zombie or the gas tank of a car."

Or a human, in the gravest extreme, Grace thought.

"If I do lab work, can I get college credits?" asked Carl.

"What's this?" asked Ben.

"I'd like to see whether elevated bilirubin levels have any effect on Z-Factor since we have blood samples from the corpse Dr. Crown brought from D.C. Elevated bilirubin might be protective against an autoimmune disease like lupus. Maybe it is protective against Z-Factor," explained Carl.

"Bilirubin. That's the pigment that turns babies yellow," said Julia.

"Right," said Carl. "It's a by-product of normal heme catabolism when your body gets rid of old red blood cells containing hemoglobin. Sometimes an elevated level indicates disease, but in cases like Gilbert's Syndrome, it seems to protect against heart disease and maybe even lupus."

"Did you think of that?" Julia asked Carl.

"No, mom. Dr. Waters did. But she said it would be fine with her if she supervised my work."

"I'm sure we can work something out," said Ben. "We'll make sure your education doesn't suffer."

"Grace, that's a good idea," said Jack. "More than that, we should look at all the anomaly studies."

IN THE END, the bilirubin studies went nowhere. The blood tests did not indicate any resistance. Carl eventually verified that two people with Gilbert's Syndrome had been bitten. They both had sickened and died. But the research team kept looking for anomalies.

Zombie Apocalypse: The Origin

Bitten

Month Four
Homewood Compound

YOU can't come home again. His father's words rang in his head all week, persistent as a throbbing headache. Claire Landi touched his arm. He bent down to let his lips meet hers for a quick kiss. Tom Peters suddenly felt a little better.

"Are you watching the touch football game?" he asked. "We want to make the newcomers feel at home."

"I'd love to see you trounce the new boys, but I have volleyball practice." It was late spring, already hot. She was dressed all in white: shorts, sneakers, and a cotton T-shirt with the sleeves of her dark blue jacket tied around her waist. Her clothes were modest as athletic wear goes, but there was no hiding her great figure.

"So, you think we're going to beat them?"

"Definitely." She smiled and smoothed a stray strand of auburn hair from her face, all the while keeping her blue eyes fixed on his.

Tom's heart skipped a beat. It had been weeks since he had seen her smile. She glanced over his shoulder, and her smile faded.

Tom wheeled around as the newcomers, Fred Murray and two boys from what was left of the neighboring town, moved toward them. "We're gonna f'n' cream 'em." The boys amped up the volume with more boasting peppered with a stream of f-bombs.

"Would you mind cleaning up the language?" Tom's voice was just loud enough for all of them to hear, but it didn't rise to the level of a shout. He instantly saw it was a bad move. Great, he thought. The bastard is coming this way. Tom watched Fred strut for the benefit of his friends. Fred was Tom's height, about six feet one, and he was fit. Tom figured they were evenly matched.

Tom had seen Fred pick fights before. As soon as Fred took control of the conversation, hostilities escalated. Six months ago, Fred started in on Glen Anderson. He complimented him on his T-shirt and asked him where he bought it. The questions continued and then turned into veiled ugly insults until Glen lashed back. Then Fred dropped the hammer,

"Gleeeen, when was the last time someone whooped your ass?"

"Hi, my name is Fred Murray. What's your name?" Ignoring Tom, he extended his hand to Claire, smirking at her.

"I know who you are." Claire's eyes narrowed. "Six months ago, you goaded Glen Anderson into taking the first swing. Cheap shot about his father's fatal car accident. Then you pounded him. Here you are again, looking for trouble. Doesn't everyone already have enough to deal with after the outbreak?"

The corners of Fred's mouth turned up slightly. He seemed to be enjoying himself. He turned to Tom. "Nice shoes. Where did you get them?"

Tom said nothing. The hell with Fred's pseudo-friendly banter. He wasn't about to play Fred's game. If this was going to end in a fight, it might as well start right now.

"We're having a private conversation," Tom retorted. "I'll see you on the field."

"That's right," affirmed Claire. "Move along."

Fred's face dissolved in confusion, and he looked away. But he wasn't ready to give up. Fred gave Claire a side-long glance and stepped closer, almost touching her body with his. "You didn't answer my question, sweetie."

Tom tensed, ready for action, and took a step closer to Fred. Claire reached out and gently touched his arm as if to say, I've got this.

"I'm not your sweetie, sonny. We asked you to move along, but instead, you're in my space, and I'm feeling harassed. Now that you know that step back."

"Or what?" Fred spat.

"Or I'll report you to Coach Landi." Claire's eyes held a challenge.

Fred didn't move. "So, you'll report me to the coach? Who do you think you are? Besides, what are you going to tell him?" Fred's face became a mask of piety.

Claire didn't budge. If anything, she inched a little closer. "Save it. I'll give him a play-by-play of your dominance display."

Fred took a step back and put his hands in front of his chest, palms out, in a gesture of mock innocence. "What makes you think he'll believe you? I was just trying to be friendly."

"You aren't being friendly. You're being a jerk. And I have a feeling my dad will believe me since he's the one who taught me about guys like you."

"So, Coach Mark Landi is your father, and you're going to run to Daddy?" Fred retorted. But his smirk was gone.

Claire gave him a look of disgust. "We took your group in yesterday because you agreed to play by our rules. You're already starting trouble and trying to push people around. Where do you think you can go if you can't get along here?"

Fred scowled, but his face gradually looked more serious. Tom thought Claire's words might have hit their target.

Claire continued, "One hundred sixty-seven people. We're all that's left of two towns and everyone within a ten-mile radius. We're lucky we have a strong gate around this high school and that zombies haven't found us, and I hope they never do. And for your information, Mark Landi is my father. He is the coach, and he also leads this community. But you already know that."

"Yeah, sorry." He shrugged and walked away.

Claire turned to Tom and smiled mischievously, "I think I can handle a second-rate bully, but I kind of liked it that you were ready to clock him."

"If he had laid a hand on you…" But she was smiling again, and Tom found he couldn't stay angry.

Her face grew serious. "I can handle myself well enough to make him regret it, but I was outmatched if it got out of hand. I liked that you didn't try to handle it for me, yet you would have stepped up if necessary. You had my back."

"You keep saying you want to fight your own battles."

Claire said nothing for a moment. Then, "But it wasn't really my battle, was it? I thought he was using me to get to you. He was picking a fight with you."

"Oh, so now you're fighting my battles?" It was all Tom could do not to laugh out loud. Claire noticed everything. Nothing got past her.

"No, I wasn't trying to fight your battles. You won the first round. You stood up to him when you told him to move on."

Tom nodded. "But he didn't stop there."

"Then he tried to get to you through me. But he underestimated both of us. He didn't think I would stand up to him, and he didn't think you'd wait and see if I could handle his goading on my own. He thought you'd jump in and swing at him to impress me because that's the kind of guy he is. He has poor judgment, and he assumes everyone else does too. At least that's the way I see it."

Tom nodded. "That's brilliant! You are light years ahead of Fred." He looked at Claire with new admiration. She didn't like games, and she had already figured out most of them. It wasn't that she didn't know how to play; she just didn't see the point.

Somewhere behind him came a familiar shout, "Hey! Wait! Bad news!" Tom's good mood vanished.

Fred also heard the shout and walked back to them.

"Hey, guys!" Juliet's face was flushed, and her breaths came fast and heavy after her sprint across the field. She delivered her message in short, staccato spurts. "It's Homewood. No game today. Check fences."

Tom asked for all of them. "What about Homewood?"

Juliet took a few deep breaths and pushed back her dark, disheveled hair. "It just came over the radio. Zombies broke through. The survivors are running. I have cousins in Homewood. Hope they're okay." Juliet had already lost her parents to the outbreak, and now her cousins were missing.

Claire turned to Tom and buried her head in his chest.

"My parents live in Homewood," said Tom. "Glen's mother lives in Homewood too." Homewood was only fifteen miles away. Almost everyone here knew someone or had family in Homewood.

"My dad's in Homewood," Fred murmured.

Juliet's brown eyes turned to deep pools of sympathy. "Oh, I'm sorry. I didn't know..."

"Thanks for finding us with the news," said Claire. "Come on, Juliet. Let's see if there's anything we can do to help make room for more refugees." She gave Tom's arm a supportive squeeze, put on her jacket, and walked down the field with Juliet to find her father.

Tom watched her go, her lean, strong legs moving with determined strides. "Fred, let's get the guys and check the fences."

TEN football players. That was all that was left of the two football teams from the community's high schools. The rest of the guys were on the field getting ready for a friendly game of touch football that wouldn't happen. But the three newcomers would come in handy today.

Four months ago, when the outbreak began, it was a holiday, and school was out. The disease tore through all the surrounding communities. Parents realized that this high school, surrounded by six acres of land, could be made safer than their homes. They fortified the fences, supplied the school, and sent as many kids as possible to live under the protection of the surviving teachers and adult volunteers. Homewood started having trouble two days ago, and more children were sent here.

"You say your dad is in Homewood?" Tom asked as they jogged to the field.

"Yup."

"Not your mom?"

"Nope."

"Divorced?"

"No, she died."

Tom was sorry he started this. But now he couldn't stop himself from asking, "Zombies?"

"Drunk driver. Glen's dad. My mom was driving. His dad plowed into the driver's side."

Tom was taken aback. Glen never talked about what happened to his father. The fight with Glen hadn't been the random act of a bully. Fred was reacting badly to a fresh wound. In the days of the iPhone, Tom could have Googled it. But there weren't even newspapers anymore. The news came by word-of-mouth or by radio if you had a generator and some equipment. This information almost made Fred's reaction understandable, but only almost.

"Not Glen's fault," said Tom.

"I know. Not proud of that. Glen didn't even know who I was."

"Glen's a good guy."

"So people told me. After."

"That's not the way to try to take control when your world is falling apart. I'm sorry about your mom, though."

Fred stumbled and righted himself. "Sorry about Glen. Sorry about how I acted just now. Sorry about your parents. Sorry about my dad, too. Seems I can't stop feeling sorry."

Tom wanted to believe him. He couldn't put his finger on it, but there was something about the way Fred talked that made it hard to trust him. His apology sounded sincere at first, but he delivered the last line as if he had rehearsed it. Tom decided to let it go; Fred had been through enough.

"Forget it. None of us is at his best. But we need the best you can manage."

Tom heard Fred exhale a sigh as if a weight had been lifted off his shoulders, and Tom picked up the pace.

But even the faster pace couldn't stop Tom from thinking about the last time he spoke to his parents. It was a week ago when it was their turn on the radio. His father's last words haunted him. *You can't come home again. I don't know how much longer we can hold out. Never forget, we love you, son.*

CLAIRE smelled the zombie, but she couldn't see it or hear it.

So did Linda, and she let out a whimper.

Claire's stomach clenched, but she took the young girl's hand in a warm clasp and gave it a gentle squeeze. She recalled what her dad had taught her: *They want your courage, however thin, not your turmoil, however real.*

Linda whimpered again.

This is why you don't bring a sheltered seven-year-old on a zombie mission, Claire thought. Linda looked up to her and had been her little shadow ever since she arrived at the camp. But this wasn't a zombie mission. This was a routine run to the storeroom, within the compound's boundaries, and it was supposed to be clear. They had never had a zombie in the compound before, and only a few people were authorized to enter the storeroom. She had come with her dad, and they had divided the supply list. He was already at the far end of the room. If she yelled for him, she would give away her position, and if her dad responded, he'd give away his position.

"Claire..." Linda pleaded softly.

Claire leaned down and whispered: "Shhh. Stay behind me and hang onto me." Claire brushed aside Linda's long blond hair; her eyes were wide and brimming. A tear coursed its way down Linda's cheek. Claire felt new resolve as she dabbed it away with the hem of her jacket.

"Where's your gun?" whispered Linda.

"In the armory," Clair replied softly. "*Shhh.*" Claire hadn't thought she'd need her gun in the compound, and now she regretted she hadn't signed out her Sig Sauer P226 9mm pistol.

Claire moved Linda's hands to the pleat in the back of her jacket and drew her Bowie knife from its sheath with her right hand. She used her left hand as a guide along the wall as they made their way down the aisle to the only switch that still worked. Electricity was precious, only for emergencies, since they only had a small generator. Flashlights and batteries were only for outside the compound, where it wasn't safe. But now, even the compound wasn't safe. Claire didn't want to be surprised in the dark. If she could get to the light switch, they'd have an easy job of sending the zombie to its final grave. She figured she'd flip the switch and yell *zombie*!

The smell of rot filled her nostrils, but she saw nothing and heard nothing. Her hand inched along the wall until she hit the edge. The switch was just around the corner to her left. She peeked around the corner and saw nothing but the coat rack and a dim room. She turned around and transferred the knife to her left hand. With her right hand, she groped for the switch while she scanned the storeroom for any sign of motion, ready for action the moment the lights came on. Just as her right hand reached the plastic cover plate for the switch, she felt a large, cold, strong hand close over hers. She tried to wrench her hand free, but the grip was too strong. Claire's eyes widened in terror, and she screamed.

"Linda, run!" Claire shouted. The zombie rounded the corner, partly pulled by Claire as she tried to free her hand. Claire drew a sharp breath. It was Mr. Bailey. She knew him by his shirt and his overall size. Three days ago, he had been at Sunday mass, a dashing grandfather. Now, he was bloated and had large blisters where gases had built up under his skin. Foul fluid leaked from his eyes, nose, ears, and mouth. The odor of death surrounded him. He moaned and gnashed his teeth, lunging for her throat as he slammed her left side against the wall, pinning her knife hand. Claire stepped back, nearly toppling Linda, who still clung to her in terror.

Linda screamed: "Zombie, *zombie*, help! *Coach Landi, help!*"

Claire pushed herself away from the wall and tried to shove Mr. Bailey back to get a chance to drive her blade into his head. In life, he had been six feet two inches and around 220 pounds, a fit, powerfully built man. Claire was a strong gymnast, but she was seventeen years old and five feet five; she was no match for him. He threw her around like a rag doll. She tried to twist her right hand upward through his thumb, but he was too strong, and zombies didn't feel pain. She kept struggling, careful to avoid his head, and managed to knock him slightly off balance to her left, but he held on tight. She still couldn't pull free or get in position to use her blade properly.

"Coming!" yelled her father from across the storeroom.

Claire heard cans being knocked over in the next aisle. Mr. Bailey's head whipped around, and he used his other hand to grab for Linda.

"*No!*" shouted Linda. She released her hold on Claire's jacket and darted through the opening Claire had made on her right.

"Run, Linda! Run and warn the others," yelled Claire.

Linda looked back, her face wet with tears. "Claire!"

"*Go!*"

Linda turned and ran, her blond hair streaming behind her.

Claire wrestled her opponent. The zombie grabbed her left arm just as her blade neared his head. He wasn't trying to defend himself; he was simply trying to bite her arm. Mr. Bailey towered over her. She used all her strength to resist him, but it only moved him back a half step. It was no use. His face drew closer.

"I'm here," her dad said as he drove his blade through Mr. Bailey's eye.

Mr. Bailey slumped to the ground. As he fell, he released Claire's left arm, but he still held her right hand. Her dad pressed his foot on Mr. Bailey's chest until he stopped writhing. Claire pried the zombie's powerful fingers open. When she was done, she looked up at her dad. Her relief gave way to horror.

"*Behind you!*"

Mrs. Bailey bit her father's left triceps. Her dad whirled and plunged his blade through her left temple. She fell to the ground in a heap, her matted hair strewn around her bloated, damaged head. Claire barely recognized her. Mrs. Bailey was always carefully groomed. She often said, "We have to keep up our standards; it's good for everyone's spirits." She would have hated to see herself this way.

Claire shuddered. She pulled herself up and ran to her dad. "Let me see."

He turned his arm toward her. Claire gasped. The flesh was torn and wet with blood and zombie slobber. "*Dad...*"

"Claire, it's no one's fault. We did our best." He walked to the switch and turned on the lights. "Let's make sure we are really alone this time."

"It's my fault. I should have checked behind the coat rack."

Her dad smiled ruefully and shook his head. "You would have still been surprised and outmatched. No one is to blame. I thought the storeroom was safe, too, until I heard your screams."

She looked at the wound again and swayed slightly. Her heart thudded against her chest. She tried not to give way to panic.

"Lift your knees to your chest, one at a time. It will keep your blood pumping to your head. We still have work to do." Her dad's voice was relaxed and gentle.

Claire nodded and obeyed, even as she felt tears welling in her eyes. She could see Mrs. Bailey's teeth marks. Her mother had died a horrible death. Within six hours, her dad would have a raging fever, and he would turn before morning.

They walked through the storeroom, down the aisles of canned and dried goods the community had collected for everyone's use. There were no more zombies. The last of the epinephrine pens were strewn on the floor of one of the aisles. Cans of stew littered the floor of another aisle. Apparently, Mrs. Bailey had knocked them over as she made her way toward Claire and Linda. Everything else was in order except for the bodies of Mr. and Mrs. Bailey.

Her dad removed his backpack. "All right then. Let's get the things we came for."

"Shouldn't we get back and clean your wound?"

"We're here now, aren't we? It will just take a second. Besides, a minute or two on this wound won't make any difference."

Claire turned her head and wiped away her tears. She felt heartsick, but she simply said, "Okay, let's do it."

Her dad gathered supplies while Claire put the epinephrine and cans of stew back where they belonged. Then, they returned to the bodies.

"Dad," said Claire, "are we just going to leave them here?"

"We'll come back for them later so we can give them a proper burial."

Claire helped him straighten the bodies. They neatly arranged the Baileys' clothing over their bloated remains and put paper napkins over their faces. Claire touched their foreheads in farewell. She nearly gagged at the stench, but she kept her voice steady. "They were lovely people."

"Yes," he agreed. "They were very kind. Let's say a quick prayer."

Claire bowed her head and crossed herself with him. When they finished, she asked, "How did this happen?"

He shook his head sadly. "I don't know. Mrs. Bailey had allergies. Perhaps she had an allergic reaction. They must have come here for the epinephrine. I suspect she died here, and Mr. Bailey was either here with her at the time, or he came looking..."

Claire gave her father's arm an anxious look. She expected to see festering by now, but the bite still looked fresh. He was six feet four inches and in top shape, a former college football star and strapping veteran of the Iraq

War. He once said he had been a killing machine. Even though he was in his early forties, he was still a formidable figure: solid, without the awkwardness of her teenage friends. He became a teacher after his service. He was the high school football coach and chemistry teacher, or at least he was before the world fell apart. Now, he led their little community.

He still taught chemistry. But he also trained them in combat and led their zombie missions when they had to venture outside. They had become an efficient team of zombie killers, yet they had occasional losses. Sometime in the middle of the night, her dad would become another casualty, a zombie that needed ending.

"If we had been wearing our protective gear, you wouldn't have gotten bitten," said Claire.

He saw her watching him with concern. "Don't dwell on it. We thought it was a safe mission. We were wrong. We can't plan for every risk. It's not a moral shortcoming; it's just the human condition."

¤

"HOW LONG do you think they were there?" asked Claire as they walked to the main building.

"The Baileys?"

"Yes."

"Well, they had already changed out of the clothes they wore to mass, so I'm guessing from the condition of the bodies that it happened Sunday night or Monday morning. That would make it over two days, maybe almost three."

"Over two days. The only reason we didn't find them sooner was that they lived in the caretaker's house. But we should have checked in on them, anyway. We need to check on each other more often." Claire's voice cracked as she realized he wouldn't be there to check on anyone ever again. She still couldn't believe it.

Her dad merely nodded. "That's a good idea."

"They helped me a lot when we first got here. Mr. Bailey made an extra room for me, and Mrs. Bailey showed me how to alter clothes and make soap and yogurt. I liked them."

"I know. They were happy to do it; they liked you. They liked you a lot. They would want you to remember them at their best, helping you when you needed them. That's who they were."

Claire said nothing for a while and then mustered the courage to ask him. "Will you sleep in the box tonight?"

"Of course. That's why we built it. I'm lucky we did."

They called it the box, but it was more like a nice guest room with a viewer slat in the only door. They had used it twice so far when they had been lucky enough to bring someone back who was wounded yet still alive. Three times, if you counted the time Coach Landi suffered a dry bite and gave them all a scare. This time, it was definitely not a dry bite.

Funny what passed for luck these days. Having basic food and shelter was lucky. Not being ripped to shreds and eaten alive, that was lucky. Not being bitten and dragged away to turn without someone to end you. That was lucky, too. The bitten that made it back alive could be near their friends, eat with them, and then spend their last hours in the box. When they turned, the ender, a volunteer, shot the new zombie through the head from the open slats in the door viewer.

She searched his face. "Who…"

Her dad gave her a gentle smile. "We have a plan. Frank Paulson will end me, and then he'll take over. He's the most knowledgeable teacher and leader we have."

No, you are, Claire thought as her eyes welled with tears, *and I'm going to lose you.*

AS THEY approached the main school building, they saw a small group running away from it, and they heard shouts of alarm.

"Oh, no," groaned Claire. "Trouble here, too."

Claire and her dad ran toward the voices. As they drew closer, they realized the shouts were for them. Shouts of greeting and relief.

Tom came at them in a flat-out run, scooped Claire up in his arms, and twirled her around. "You don't know how glad I am to see you. We were just setting out to help. Linda said..."

But instead of matching his relief, Claire's body tensed.

"What is it?" Tom asked.

"My dad. Mrs. Bailey bit him..."

Tom put her down just as Juliet, Glen, and Mr. Paulson caught up with them.

"Coach Landi, may I take a look at that?" asked Tom.

Her dad turned his left arm so Tom could get a good look. Tom examined the undressed wound and shook his head. His face clouded over. "This looks bad."

"There's no use hiding from reality," her dad said.

Frank Paulson examined it, too. Claire saw his look of shock, and he seemed to struggle to keep his voice steady. "It's a bad one. Let's get it cleaned up. Then let's get something to eat." He looked at her father. "Mark, let's hope we're right."

Her father smiled weakly. "I'm an optimist."

Claire wanted to ask them what they meant by that, but Tom took her arm and coaxed her inside.

ONCE inside the building, Frank Paulson cleaned the wound while Claire and Tom watched. It was odd, though. He never wasted antibiotics on people who had been bitten by a zombie, but Mr. Paulson gave her dad an injection. Out of respect, Claire guessed.

"We're posting a notice," her dad said. "There's a 9:00 p.m. emergency meeting in the auditorium. You'd better go now to get ready for 6:00 p.m. dinner."

Claire cleaned off the zombie slobber, changed outfits, put her soiled clothes in the decontamination bag for burning, and signed out her Sig Sauer. Then she sought out Linda to assure the little girl that she was all right. She explained how her father had rescued her and that the zombies had been the Baileys, not outsiders. She answered Linda's persistent questions but left out the part about Mrs. Bailey biting her dad. She also left out the news about Homewood.

By the time they sat down for 6:00 p.m. dinner in the cafeteria, news of her dad's wound had swept through the adults in the community. The adults who didn't prepare dinner in private joined them in the cafeteria, and the mood was heavy.

After dinner, they put the youngsters to bed. The community ran on a schedule. Everyone was up by 7 a.m., and everyone had chores, starting with making one's bed. Children and teenagers had school, homework, and mandatory exercise. Teenagers also had a minimum of 30 minutes of daily combat training. Everyone could take a nap after school if they needed it. Pre-teens got ready for bed at 8:00 p.m., and bedtime was 8:30 p.m. Teenagers had to turn in by 10:00 p.m. No exceptions.

As Tom walked toward the assembly hall, he saw Fred and Glen deep in conversation. *Good*, he thought. Fred must be apologizing. He walked closer.

"I thought you Catholics were all about forgiveness," said Fred, his voice dripping with contempt.

"We're not Spaniels," Glen retorted. "There's no need to forgive where there's no remorse and no commitment to change."

This didn't sound like it was going well. Tom thought he'd better let them work it out and sought out Claire.

"How are you doing?"

"I'm okay," lied Claire. She didn't tell him that she was still scared out of her mind and carrying her gun, but she offered this much: "I got schooled. I learned that if a fresh adult male zombie gets the jump on me, I might not survive. And my dad won't be around to save me next time." Her eyes brimmed with tears again.

"It could have been any of us."

"I know. But combat training was starting to make me forget that we can get hemmed in and that anyone can get bitten." Claire thought about that for a moment. "I think training made me feel overconfident. I'm sad about my dad. He's talking to Mr. Paulson now, but I have to get back to him." Claire sighed heavily and asked, "What's that all about?" She nodded in Fred and Glen's direction.

Claire's eyes widened in surprise as Tom told her about his earlier conversation with Fred. She knew Glen's father died in a post-outbreak car crash, but this was the first time she'd heard the details. She had no idea Fred and his mother were involved.

"Let's ask Glen how their conversation went. He's headed this way," Tom said as he glanced into the distance behind Claire.

She turned to see Glen approaching rapidly. Fred glowered behind him. He stood stone still. When Fred saw where Glen was headed, he spun around and walked quickly in the other direction.

"Do you believe that guy?" Glen began. "It's all I can stand to be in the same room with him." Glen's lean six-foot frame seemed tense with pent-up energy. His usually mild features were dark with anger.

"Glen, I'm sorry about your dad, but he lost his mom too..." Tom said.

"What did he tell you?" Glen asked.

Tom told him about their conversation and ended, "I'm sorry that he aired your personal life. I wasn't trying to pry, but he told me his mom had died, and I asked him how it happened."

Glen looked even angrier, and a muscle around his right jaw muscle throbbed. Glen took a deep breath and reverted to Coach Landi's teaching to summarize the situation. "He *lied*. I knew who he was when he baited me a few months ago; I knew exactly who I was swinging at. My dad didn't drink. Fred and his mom had blood alcohol levels over 0.8; they had been at a party and were both legally drunk. His mom was speeding and ran a red light. She plowed into the driver's side of my dad's car. My dad's airbag deployed, but part of the door lodged in his side. My dad died two days later of the injuries. The hospital staff, what remained of them, had to end him after he turned. Fred's airbag deployed, and he was bruised but otherwise uninjured. His mom's defective Takata airbag deployed, but when the propellant wafers ignited, it was with explosive force. A piece of the metal cartridge lodged in her neck. She turned in the car. Fortunately, she was still pinned to her seat by the airbag and couldn't bite Fred. A bystander at the scene ended her."

Tom and Claire were speechless.

"You believe me, don't you?" he asked plaintively.

"No question," responded Tom immediately. "And I can see why you didn't want to talk about it."

Glen's jaw muscles relaxed, and then he suddenly deflated. "I can't believe this is happening. He maligned my dad and told everyone it was his fault. I wish he never came here."

Tom didn't know what to say to that. They were stuck with Fred.

"If I turn, don't end me until I bite him," said Claire.

Glen managed a small laugh. "I'm glad I have loyal friends."

HER father's last speech was short. He turned his leadership over to Mr. Paulson and then talked about how proud he was of everyone who kept hope alive, singled out a few people with kind words of encouragement, and ended with a final quip for his students. "I'm impressed with how much your people skills have grown now that you can't use the internet or social media."

Everyone either laughed or nodded or both.

Mr. Paulson took over. "We will keep to our schedules. We will continue with chores, homework, and training. I'll have another short announcement after breakfast at 8:00 a.m. tomorrow here in the auditorium. Get a good night's sleep, everybody."

Claire had to admit that Frank Paulson sounded like a leader. He had always taken a back seat to her dad, but now her dad faded into the background and supported him. She was amazed at how quickly leadership transformed and how easily everyone seemed to accept it. All their hard work to make them a community paid off in this crisis.

Frank Paulson and her dad left the podium, and everyone filed out of the assembly hall.

Zombie Apocalypse: The Origin

Ancestors

Outbreak Compound, Virginia

DR. Benjamin Lieber strode past the men in Colonel Crown's office, slapped his hand on the desk, and exclaimed, "We hit the jackpot! Look at the genetic workup on this couple."

Jack looked at the blood work. There appeared to be some common DNA markers. "They're cousins?"

"No. At least not close enough to matter, maybe eighth cousins or something like that. Their ancestors came from the same town in Italy."

Jack still didn't see what Ben meant. "Help me out. I'm not a geneticist. What am I looking for? Are they both still alive?"

"She's not, but…"

"Wait, how do you know she's not alive?"

"Medical records. The wife died of Huntington's disease three years ago. There's no cure."

"I see why she had the genetic workup, but why did he? That's unusual."

"That's just it. There's a daughter. The daughter had the full genetic workup, and the father did, too. That often happens with families when something like this happens. They want to know exactly what it is they are passing on to their children. It turns out the daughter is in the clear."

"The daughter had a fifty-fifty chance. She won't get Huntington's disease, and she won't pass the gene on to any of her children if she ever has any. Lucky girl."

"Very. Because she inherited a rare gene from both parents, just as her parents did from their parents."

"What is that?"

"The ancestors of the mother, father, and daughter survived the plague. Both the surviving father and daughter carry a gene that may be protective against the Z-Factor virus."

"Like that elderly monk who we think survived a zombie bite?"

"Yes, but he died of heart failure, and we couldn't verify that he had been bitten."

"Two new prospects," said Jack.

"We got lucky," nodded Ben. "Now comes the hard part."

"Right." Jack Crown stood up, his six-foot-four-inch frame of trained muscle a formidable sight. "Now we have to find them and get them back here in one piece."

Michael K. Clancy

Inheritance

Homewood Compound

CLAIRE heard a twig snap behind her and whirled around with her left hand at her chest while her right hand firmly grabbed her pistol grip. Her wrist was straight as she pulled her gun straight up. She kept her wrist in a straight line with her forearm. She rotated her arm, keeping her shoulder down and slightly forward as she drew back the slide and released it, cocking the hammer and chambering a round. In a flash, she was in a perfect close-contact firing position.

"Hey! Take it easy, Annie Oakley. What are you doing up so early?"

Claire paled. "Sorry, Tom. Why didn't you announce yourself?" She pointed the gun in a safe direction, removed her finger from the trigger, and removed the magazine by pulling back on the slide. She locked it using the slide catch lever. Then she removed the round in the chamber. She checked the chamber again physically and visually to be sure it was empty. Satisfied, she released the slide. Then she pushed down on the decocking lever. Now that her weapon was safe, she holstered it. "What are *you* doing up and about at 6 a.m.?"

"Same thing you are. I'm on my way to the box to see if Mr. Paulson needs help with your dad's body." He scanned her face. "Hey, I didn't mean to sneak up on you; I was about to hail you, but you drew too fast for me."

"Sorry, I'm still jumpy."

"Jumpy is good. I'd rather you were safe than sorry."

"I'd rather it were last year when we didn't need guns."

"Me too. But it's not."

They entered the field house, which held the box. It also held a separate cubicle, which had a radio transmitter and receiver. The door to the box was wide open, and they saw no one. Claire drew her gun again and removed the safety. There was no one inside. No blood, no sign of a struggle.

"Do you think Mr. Paulson already removed him for burial?"

"No," said Tom. "Not this early. Something's not right."

He didn't have to say what they were both thinking. Frank Paulson had let her dad go. Perhaps he had let him loose in the woods.

They heard a crackling sound, electronic static coming from the radio cubicle. They walked to the half-windowed door and looked through the glass. Mr. Paulson sat in the operator's chair, and three feet behind him loomed the tall figure of her father.

Claire thought she would get a better shot if she opened the door instead of shooting through the glass. She drew and prepared her weapon. Then she turned the knob and pushed. The door creaked in protest. Both Frank Paulson and her dad looked in her direction.

"*Stop!* I'm all right," shouted her dad.

Claire's hands shook as she turned her gun away from her dad and made her weapon safe again. For the second time that day, she holstered her gun after nearly blowing away someone she loved. It wasn't quite 6:10 a.m.

"Come in! Come in and listen to this!" Mr. Paulson sounded elated.

"...so, we need him and the daughter here as soon as possible. He's the second one of the Plague survivors' descendants to show no signs after a bite. We're glad you don't need a Band-

Aid buggy. We look forward to meeting Coach Zombie. Please confirm. Over." The voice on the radio was crisp and clear.

Mr. Paulson toggled a switch. "10-4. He'll start for you this morning, and you'll meet him on the road, if possible. He's bringing four additional passengers. Over."

"Copy that. Over and out."

"I didn't know you knew radio broadcast lingo, Mr. Paulson," said Tom.

"I don't. Not really. Close enough, though. I know that Band-Aid buggy means ambulance, and I sort of know how to sign off. The main thing is we can communicate."

"Who was that?" asked Claire.

"Dr. Benjamin Lieber. He heads a team of military and medical doctors holed up in a research compound," responded her father. "They've set up a research center and mobilized medical personnel and other workers. Looking for a cure. They are amply supplied and heavily defended."

Claire carefully looked her dad over. He seemed perfectly fine. "Dad, are you okay? Do you have a fever?"

"No, I've never felt better."

"He called you Coach Zombie," said Tom.

Claire and Tom exchanged looks, trying not to laugh.

Something suddenly dawned on Claire, and she turned to Frank Paulson. "*You knew*. That's why you gave my dad antibiotics."

Mr. Paulson gave a slight shrug. "I didn't know, but we had hope. Do you remember the dry bite? We called it that, even though nobody ever heard of a dry bite. Sometimes, a snake bite is dry, a bite without venom. But so far, we haven't heard of a dry zombie bite."

"Yes, of course, I remember."

"It was just a scratch, though, and we couldn't be sure. This one was a wet bite."

"Yes, so how..."

"Your dad and a late Franciscan monk are the only two people in the world that we know of who have been bitten and haven't shown any symptoms. We're not one hundred percent sure about the monk, and in any case, he died of old age. They want to see your father as soon as possible."

"Are you saying he's immune?" asked Claire.

"We don't know for sure. That's why they want him at the Compound."

"That's right," said her dad. "No sluffing off on your science homework."

"Well then, what do you think are the odds?" asked Tom.

"We're trying to find out. Father Matteo, a Franciscan monk, was the other plague descendant they found. We have common ancestors from the same town in Italy. They survived the black plague, even though they tended to their sick relatives and nursed their sick neighbors. Our genetic studies show we inherited a mutated gene, CCR5, delta 32. This mutation may have protected our ancestors from the black plague. This same mutation may provide a blocking mechanism that prevents the zombie virus from binding to our blood cells. Father Matteo inherited the same mutation from both of his parents, too."

"But you said both parents. Mom..." asked Claire.

"That's just it," replied her father, "your mom had the mutation, and I have it. You do, too."

"Mom had it? Why didn't anyone tell us about this before?"

"It wasn't important. Who gets the plague today? They probably did tell me, but I wasn't interested in everything they said at the time. I had Huntington's on my mind. I just wanted to know whether you had inherited the gene and to make sure you hadn't inherited anything bad from me. I wasn't thinking about anything else."

"Yes," said Claire softly. Then she fell silent.

"It's immunity," declared Tom.

"No," cautioned her dad. "It's a hypothesis. Even if I'm immune—and not just resistant—we're still a long way from developing a cure."

"But it's a good start," insisted Tom.

"I'm glad you are both here," said her dad. "I would like the two of you and Juliet and Glen to come with me to the compound. Consider it a zombie mission. 300 miles. Before the outbreak, it would have been around a six-hour drive. Now, we have no idea how many obstacles we'll find or how dangerous it will be."

Tom and Claire exchanged glances.

Claire looked back at her dad and said, "Linda's parents are in Homewood. Who will take care of her if I go?"

Mr. Paulson answered. "I spoke with Mrs. Burns last night. If you agree to go, she will be happy to take care of Linda while you're gone."

"Thanks," said Claire. Mrs. Burns was a good choice. It's who she would have picked.

"I'll go," said Tom.

"Good," said her father. He assessed Tom and seemed satisfied. "Please tell Glen and Juliet that I'm well and ask them to come here to see us. Then get some breakfast, pack, and say your goodbyes. We'll inform the community after breakfast, and we'll start for the compound at 9:00 a.m."

Tom left, and her dad pulled her aside. "Claire, you don't look happy. What are you thinking?"

"Dad, I'm grateful you're alive."

"But..."

"It's Mom. I feel like I let Mom down."

"Honey, nothing that happened to your mother is anyone's fault."

"I know. It's just that I had been thinking how glad I was that I didn't inherit the gene for Huntington's from her. I was grateful for something I did not want and did not have."

"You're a lot like her. You inherited all of her great qualities."

"You've always told me that. But I was so busy being relieved about what she didn't give me that I didn't appreciate what she did give me."

"Well, that's a relief."

"What?"

"My daughter isn't a zombie. She has normal, complicated human feelings."

Claire smiled and even managed a small laugh.

"You're young. It's only natural to have complicated feelings about illness and death. This is not the world I would have chosen for you."

"But it's the one we live in."

CLAIRE checked on Linda in the girls' dormitory. Claire always thought that Linda was completely dependent on her, so she was surprised to see her playing Monopoly with three other girls. Linda had made more friends than Claire realized.

"I'll miss you a lot, but I'm glad to be here with my friends," said Linda.

"Oh, so you don't care that I'm going away?" teased Claire.

"You'll have Tom to take care of you. And your dad and Juliet and Glen." The corners of her mouth turned down slightly. Linda lowered her head and tugged on the sleeve of her blouse.

"Yes, but I'll think of you every single day. Stay safe, study, and listen to Mrs. Burns. I won't be here for the Baileys' burial, so say an extra prayer for them. I love you a lot, you know."

"Okay," said Linda. She gave Claire a plaintive look. "They didn't mean to be zombies."

"No, they didn't. There's something else you can do for me."

"What?" Linda asked, eager to help.

"Fold my clothes from the laundry. They are in the dryer. That way, I'll have something clean to wear when I get back."

Linda's face brightened. "I'll keep them in my drawer."

"Thanks. It will make me feel better knowing you are taking care of my things."

"Maybe I can go home and visit Mom and Dad next week."

"That's up to Mr. Paulson and Mrs. Burns." They still hadn't told the younger children about Homewood. There had been no further communication since yesterday afternoon, and with luck, some or all the parents would show up sometime today. If not, they'd deal with telling the children after that. "Now give me a hug."

Linda looked up and threw her arms around Claire. "Come back from your zombie mission safe and sound."

Claire stood up and shouldered her backpack. She gave Linda a final kiss on the cheek. As she walked away, she said a silent prayer for Linda's parents. *I hope you're all right.*

"CLAIRE, how is she settling in?" asked Mrs. Burns.

Claire removed her backpack and rested it on the floor. "Linda seems to be adjusting. I can't thank you enough."

"Do you have everything you need?"

"I think so. We should be fine. It's 300 miles. Maybe we can cover it in six hours." But they both knew any trip outside the fences was dangerous, and this was the longest trip anyone had taken in months. They had no way of knowing whether the roads were clear, and they had to rely on paper maps. Claire missed the days of GPS.

Mrs. Burns said goodbye and hurried off to manage her day. Out of the corner of Claire's eye, she saw Mrs. Treadwell moving quickly in her direction. It was too late to avoid her.

"I heard you are going away for a couple of days. I'll take care of Linda as if she were my own daughter," said Mrs. Treadwell.

Claire stiffened. "Mrs. Burns is taking charge of her, but of course, an extra pair of eyes always helps."

Mrs. Treadwell looked crestfallen. "My little Deirdre still screams and cries after it gets dark."

A chill raced up Claire's spine.

"I went to her grave and begged her to stop."

Claire said nothing.

Mrs. Treadwell looked up, her face a mask of pain. "I know she's dead. I'm not crazy…"

"You're mourning her," Claire said. "Please talk to Mr. Paulson again." People who lost loved ones often thought they heard them or caught a glimpse of them. Grief was a powerful emotion that played tricks on the mind. The outbreak was bad enough, but grief was so common and so deep that it was an epidemic.

The sides of Mrs. Treadwell's mouth twitched upward, and she nodded her head slowly. "I will."

"I hear you play backgammon. You have a board." Claire hoped that giving her something to do might help.

"Yes…"

"Could you teach Linda and the other girls to play?"

"Yes, I could do that," Mrs. Treadwell said a little too eagerly. "I don't want to make them sad, though. I'll have to act like I'm okay."

"I've watched you around the children. You cover it up well when you're around them."

"I have to do it for them," Mrs. Treadwell explained. She sounded as if she were trying to convince herself. "They need adults to be dependable."

We all have to fake feeling okay, Claire thought. "Do it for them," she said aloud. She gave Mrs. Treadwell a quick hug. This wasn't a problem that had a simple solution, and Claire was out of time. She scooped up her backpack and hurried off to the car.

¤

TOM couldn't see Claire. The Jeep Grand Cherokee was parked in front of the gate 100 yards away, past a couple of rows of cars and in plain view. They had packed almost everything half an hour ago, and then Tom drove it to the main gate. Their backpacks, road armor, and road weapons were already neatly stowed. They had each signed out extra handguns and knives. Tom signed out four sharp-pointed spear-like steel weapons, flashlights, and other gear for the entire group. Claire left the building three minutes ago, and he had handed her the keys so that she could open the rear door to check the packing and make sure everything was tied down and stable. Juliet, Glen, and Claire's father were back in the building, saying their final goodbyes.

"Claire," he shouted. "How does it look?" No response. Where was she? She couldn't be inside the building. If she had doubled back, he would have seen her. She must be inside the Jeep already, unable to hear him.

Tom was itching to get on the road, but he waited outside the building for the others. They had a full tank of precious gas. Theoretically, that should take them 700 miles, enough to drive to the compound and back if they were lucky. Tom had stowed a spare five-gallon can of gas, just in case.

Where was Claire?

Tom walked toward the Jeep. He heard Claire scream, a mixture of rage, fear, and pain. His heart beat furiously as he ran toward the sound. Then he heard a shot, and Claire screamed again. Then he heard a shout behind him.

"Claire! Tom!"

Tom glanced behind and saw Claire's father with Frank Paulson, Glen, and Juliet hard on his heels.

Tom reached the front of the car. Claire was on the ground, flat on her back. She struggled with Fred, who was on top of her, pinning her down. Fred tried to wrest the gun from Claire's hands. Tom drew his gun, put it to Fred's temple, and pulled the trigger. Fred's head jerked away. Tom saw a puff of smoke and could smell Fred's flesh and burnt powder.

The bullet had already traveled through Fred's brain and exited the other side of his head when he slumped to the side. Claire rolled him off her and removed the gun and her hands from Fred's dead hands.

"Are you hurt?" Tom asked anxiously as he helped Claire to her feet.

The others arrived just in time to hear her reply.

"No," said Claire. "It was a wild shot. It went out past the gate, into the woods somewhere."

"What happened?"

"I had just closed up the back when he got the jump on me. He took the keys and ran around to the front. I drew my gun and made him drop the keys. They're over there on the ground. As I stooped to pick them up, he jumped on me. The gun went off as we struggled."

"That's twice in two days that your life has been in danger," said Claire's father.

"Tom, you're shaking," said Claire.

"I've never had to kill anyone before. Lots of zombies, but that's not the same thing," said Tom.

"Take some deep breaths," said Claire's father. "I'm glad you were here to help Claire. It couldn't be helped."

"We shared everything we had with him," said Claire, "and he tried to steal from us. He was even prepared to kill me to do it."

"You'd better go," said Frank Paulson. "I'll take care of the body, and I'll close the gate behind you. I hope that shot didn't attract any unwelcome visitors."

After they were settled in the Jeep, Claire's father rolled down the window and reached down to shake Frank's hand.

"I wish this had been a pleasant goodbye," said Frank. "Good luck. Don't look back. Look ahead. I hope some good comes from this."

"Good luck to you too, Frank."

As the Jeep passed through Homewood's open gate, Claire's father said, "It's 9:10 a.m., and that's behind us. Only 300 miles to go."

Zombie Apocalypse: The Origin

BOOK 4

ZOMBIES AND MEN

Volunteers

Outbreak Compound, Virginia
Two Hours Earlier

COLONEL Jack Crown, M.D. raised his voice. "I don't know the answer, so let's all be afraid."

Jack paused his lecture and assessed the faces of the thirty people in the auditorium. All of them were young, fit, and well-trained. Some met his eyes with a steady gaze. He wasn't worried about them. Others showed doubt, looked away, or shifted uncomfortably in their chairs. The psychological pressure was beginning to wear them down.

"That was our so-called government's response," Jack continued. Our approach is rational, "We don't know the answer, so let's stay calm and try to find the answer."

He assessed his audience again and saw a raised hand. "Yes," he said, nodding in its direction. "You have a question?"

Major Juan Chavez rose to his feet and stood erect. "Sir, would it help if we required those who are infected with the Z-Factor virus to wear masks?"

"Yes, Major Chavez, it would. You're in charge of enforcing the mask requirement."

The men laughed loudly. It was a welcome release.

Jack grinned as he resumed. "Based on our lending library data, most of you have read Michael Crichton's *The Andromeda Strain*, *Jurassic Park*, and *State of Fear*. The late Doctor Michael Crichton graduated from Harvard Medical School. He was a brilliant fiction author. But he was an even better medical researcher."

Someone in the audience gave a surprised murmur. Jack paused for a moment before continuing.

"In a presentation to The Independent Institute in 2005, Dr. Crichton made the following observations. He stressed that the lack of accurate information has a devastating psychological impact. At that time, he was talking about viruses such as the Asian Flu and disasters such as Chernobyl. Does anyone know how many people died due to the Chernobyl accident?"

No one volunteered an answer.

"Let me help you out. Fifty-six, according to a UN Commission. That's the number of people that used to die daily in the USA from traffic accidents. Hundreds of fake news articles on Chernobyl were published by major mainstream media such as *The New York Times*, *The Canadian Broadcasting Company*, and *United Press International*."

Jack let that sink in while he flipped over his papers.

"The long-term effects were vastly overblown. So-called experts scared the hell out of the general population. People were told their children would be born deformed and that they might be sterile. They were told to expect cancer and other diseases. People felt helpless, demoralized, and dependent on the government. They thought they'd have a much-shortened life expectancy. Tens of thousands of Ukrainians became invalids paralyzed by fear, yet none of those disastrous scenarios ever happened. They were terrorized by fake news.

False information was, in this case, worse than radiation."

"We all recall the hemorrhagic fever virus called HF3560 that infected workers in a U.S. research lab in Chile. Within three months, it had spread around the globe. Despite Dr. Crichton's 2005 warning about fear, we made the same mistake again. We crashed our economy due to a disinformation campaign. Early news reports said the virus was airborne. It wasn't."

"The virus itself was as terrifying as Ebola or Marburg. It was highly infectious. It caused hemorrhages: bleeding from the eyes and nose. Sufferers coughed up blood. Half of the infected died."

"But the virus wasn't airborne. One had to come in contact with the bodily fluids of the infected or with items contaminated with their bodily fluids such as infected needles, saliva, or bodily waste."

"Entire countries shut down trying to prevent an airborne epidemic. Quacks pushed useless treatment. Effective treatments were suppressed. Schools were shut down unnecessarily—all because of politics and an election year in the United States."

"Using CDC numbers, of the general global population, around 75,000 died of HF3560 before it was contained."

Jack continued. "Fear *paralyzed* the country due to misinformation. When you asked the average person, they overestimated the deaths by a factor of more than *one hundred thirty*. They thought ten million people had died worldwide."

Jack pressed a button, and a chart appeared on the overhead screen. "Let's look at the projection of our current problem, the Z-Factor virus."

The chart showed Z-Factor's exponential progression. The numbers looked grim. Dr. Lieber's best-case scenario for an uninformed public was that by day thirteen, there would be around 50 million zombies in the U.S. They were now in month four.

"Z-Factor is a *real* threat to mankind's survival," commented Jack. "Some people have pulled together. Others unraveled."

He pressed the button again, and a new line appeared on the graph. The progression was still fast, but the curve was flatter. If people had quickly organized and fought back—and some had—the number could have been as low as ten million. But no one knew what the numbers were like now. All of them had been in Washington, D.C. or the surrounding area when the outbreak occurred, and they all saw how society unraveled in a couple of days. By day two, they had evacuated. They were the lucky ones.

"We've all seen these numbers. Communication and feedback are poor. The reality is that we don't know how many people are infected and how many are uninfected. We have reports that people are fighting back."

Jack pressed the button again. This time, crime statistics from Chicago were compared with deaths from HF3560, the virus that was much less of a threat to mankind than so-called experts initially thought, for the concurrent period.

The chart showed that in the under-fifty-five age group, *117 more* people died from *homicide* than from HF3560.

The contrast was even starker in the under-eighteen age group. *Fourteen* children had died in *shootings,* of which four were under the age of ten. During the same period, *two* children died from HF3560.

"When people are afraid and when law enforcement breaks down, people can be a bigger threat to each other than an actual deadly disease. It's all the more tragic when the threat is wildly overestimated. In our case, the Z-Factor threat is worse than we could have imagined. But is it more terrifying than any other highly contagious, deadly illness? The suffering of victims seems shorter. But it has a horror factor because the dead rise again."

Jack saw most heads nod in agreement.

"We default to the level of our training, and we are all well trained. We've all seen the death of our comrades in arms, and we've all killed. We're a unit. We have an advantage. That's why I'm asking for volunteers to accompany me on a long-distance mission. We will configure a pair of Humvees as nine-passenger troop carriers in case there is any trouble close to the compound because of anyone seeing our departure and return. But I need seven volunteers for the long-distance mission."

Every hand in the room went up.

"That's more than I need. I'll sort it out in a minute. Put your hands down. Let me first ask if you have any questions."

Chavez stood up again. His previous levity was gone. He asked the question on everyone's mind. "Sir, why are you asking for just seven volunteers? How far is this mission?"

"We are to find and retrieve a group of five people traveling 300 miles to our facility. At sixty miles an hour, the trip would have taken them five hours before the outbreak. But we don't know what awaits them between where they are now and here. We hope to meet them on the road and fly them here. We should lift off the Merlin about an hour ahead of their departure. We're bringing a medical team and equipment. With eight soldiers, including me and the pilot and co-pilot among the soldiers, we'll still have room for five passengers and potential surprises."

Jack Crown had insisted on the Merlin when he and Dr. Lieber set up the Outbreak Compound. It was made by both the United Kingdom and Italy and had a longer range and more capacity than its American counterparts. He refused the Lockheed Martin Sikorsky line and Boeing Apaches—could anyone trust their quality control?

The Merlin utility helicopter could take thirty to forty passengers, fully equipped with a

12.7 mm machine gun. The medical gear and medical team cut down passenger capacity. The armored cockpit crew consisted of a pilot and co-pilot. In a pinch, the helicopter could be flown by a single pilot. They all knew the challenge was its limited range. It was just under 600 miles, not enough to get there and back and deal with surprises. The group they needed to pick up had to meet them partway. The helicopter's maximum speed was just over 190 miles per hour, but they'd travel at a cruise speed of about 170 miles per hour.

"There's something I'd like to add. Most of us could not take as many family members as we wanted to this compound. We've endured a strict communications blackout with those we had to leave behind. I want you to know that this mission isn't to retrieve people who pulled strings to break our protocol. The newcomers are valuable to us because two of them have a genetic anomaly that may provide resistance to the Z-Factor virus. One is an adult; the other is a teenager. The other three are teenagers, young adults. They are accompanying the others in case there's trouble."

Jack heard a gasp. He ignored it.

Everyone in the room knew what this news meant. The best protection these civilians could muster and spare were teenagers. Forces to protect civilians must be thin on the ground, and they all had—and hoped they still had—people they cared about on the outside. They were all glad this wasn't a mission to protect a connected politician, and all of them wanted to protect these kids who were willing to make what would likely be a dangerous journey.

Jack concluded, "Even though I can take just seven of you for the away team, I'm proud of all of you for volunteering for this search and rescue mission."

Zombie Apocalypse: The Origin

The Chopper

Road from Homewood to the Outbreak Compound

"STAY near the Jeep if we take a rest stop. If possible, we must stay on the route the Virginia compound transmitted to me. After our initial radio call at 6 a.m., the Virginia people sent directions and guidance. If we're lucky, staff from the medical compound—and soldiers— will intercept us via helicopter. They radioed to say they would lift off at 9:00 a.m., the same time we were due to leave the compound. But we were delayed by ten minutes." This was the first opportunity Coach Mark Landi had to explain to Claire, Tom, Glen, and Juliet that they would have an escort to Virginia.

"Why are they meeting us on the road? Why didn't they just fly to the Homewood school compound? How will they find us?" asked Glen.

"It's a problem of range. They must make it to us and back again. That means leaving some slack in case things don't go as expected. As for how they will find us, I've taped a one-foot-thick cross with yellow reflective tape on the roof of the Jeep."

"How much range do they have?" persisted Glen.

"A little under 600 miles, at least that's what the specs say. We want to get as close to them as possible in case either group has to deviate from the course or if either group somehow gets bogged down."

They each had their zombie gear. It consisted of pads for the torso and limbs. The pads were reinforced with layers of newspaper. Zombies couldn't bite through it, but the wearers could still move their joints. It was lightweight and effective. Each of them had a football helmet.

The Jeep Cherokee seated five, but it was a tight fit with their gear crammed into the floor space. Glen sat upfront with Mark; he wore Mark's Steiner 10x50 Military binoculars on a neck strap. Tom, Juliet, and Claire rode in the back, with Claire on the middle bench seat.

Mark Landi thought he could improve their odds. "Tom, take the reflective tape and scissors out of this small bag on the floor in front of you. I want each of you to tape a cross to your helmet and to the front of your breastplates. Do mine, too, please."

As the teens worked, Mark continued, "I want it to be easy for them to identify us from the air. Meanwhile, your job is to look like a happy, harmless group on their way to the next town to see relatives."

"What about the Jeep?" Mark's daughter asked.

Tom answered for Mark. "I'll drive the Jeep back, Claire. My parents will try to make their way from town to the Homewood school compound if they can." He didn't need to add *if they were still alive*. "I'll take our weapons back, too."

"Not my sidearm," said Claire, protectively touching her holster.

Not your sidearm," Tom agreed softly. "Not anyone's sidearm. But the heavy weaponry might be needed at Homewood, and it seems the Virginia people have a lot of resources."

"I wish you wouldn't go back," Claire added, her voice trembling.

"I can't give up hope. I don't want to leave you. But you'll be with your father, and this new place sounds much better protected than the Homewood school grounds."

Claire slowly nodded and then turned away from him to gaze out the window. She struggled to hold back her tears.

"It seems you and my dad have discussed this," she said without looking at him. It wasn't an accusation. It was resignation.

"We did," Mark Landi confirmed. "Tom and Glen asked to travel back together."

"I would have told you earlier," Tom explained, "but I didn't see the point unless your father agreed. He's in charge. Coach Zombie has kept us alive so far."

Coach Zombie. Claire noticed his attempt to lift her spirits. She nodded silently. Then she gathered her strength and turned her face to Tom to find that he had been watching her the entire time. She managed a small smile.

"I would do the same if the situation were reversed. I'm proud of you. I'll always be proud of you," she said.

Her father couldn't help but overhear their exchange. His heart swelled. *I'm proud of both of you*, he thought.

*****

MARK Landi snaked his way through backroads. He ran into a few cars heading in the opposite direction, toward the school. They were refugees from the overrun town. Each time, drivers rolled down their windows to ask whether the road to the school's compound was still safe. Mark asked about the road they had just traveled. It seemed both coming and going, the roads were still clear.

Mark also inquired about Tom's parents and Glen's mother. No one had news of the boys' relatives. The drivers didn't know them and had no idea how many people had made it out of town.

Claire, Tom, Juliet, and Glen kept their eyes peeled for any sign of Tom's parents or Glen's mother in case they were traveling on foot. Juliet's parents had died months ago, but she expressed hope that Glen and Tom would get news of their loved ones.

Mark slowed down as the Jeep approached a man, accompanied by two women, walking in the middle of his lane. He didn't know them, but they appeared to be refugees from town.

"Stay alert," Mark warned the teenagers. He remained wary as he rolled down his window.

"Get out of the road!" Mark shouted to the group. The women didn't move. As the man walked toward his window, Mark rolled it up.

A fourth traveler, a man, sprang out of his concealment on the side of the road and tried the Jeep's passenger side door handle next to Juliet. The doors were locked.

Juliet undid her holster and drew her gun. She kept the safety on for the moment.

Glen displayed his gun as Mark slowly moved the Jeep forward. The women on the road didn't move, and the man outside Mark's door pounded on the Jeep. Mark let the Jeep advance. The women finally stepped aside. Mark felt the Jeep brush against the man and one of the women. As soon as he was clear, Mark sped off. Once the Jeep reached the highway, Mark accelerated to 80 miles per hour.

Tom put his arm around Claire, and she put her head on his shoulder. Within minutes, her nervous energy turned to exhaustion. A sleepless night worrying about her father, the early morning revelation that her father had survived, Fred's attack and fighting off Fred, Tom's having to kill Fred, leaving Homewood, the Homewood people who had tried to—what had they tried to do: get a ride, steal the Jeep, worse?—and the news that Tom was leaving took their toll. She drifted off.

IN THE PAST HOUR—even with the short delays—they had covered 60 miles of the 300-mile trip. But Mark began to feel uneasy. When he first left the Homewood school compound, cars were moving in the opposite direction. Since the initial outbreak, traffic had dropped dramatically, but cars still had mostly safe travel on the roads and highways. His Jeep was the sole vehicle in his lane. That didn't seem too odd because traffic was sparse. But he had expected some traffic in the oncoming lanes. He hadn't seen another car for some time. How long had it been?

Mark knew his 20/20 vision should allow him to see around thirty miles ahead in these clear conditions. His 10x50 binoculars would magnify that about ten times, allowing him to see 300 miles ahead. But the road wasn't completely straight.

In the distance, eight to ten miles ahead, he could see with his naked eyes what looked to be a roadblock.

"Glen, what do you see through the binoculars?" Mark asked as he applied the brakes. The Jeep traveled 500 feet before stopping.

"Both sides of the highway are blocked off. Several cars are parked sideways across the road. A group of people seems to be standing in front of the cars." Glen was silent for a couple of seconds and continued slowly, "Coach, I don't like the look of this."

Mark took the binoculars from Glen's outstretched hands. "Everyone, put on your gear and recheck your weapons. Be ready for anything."

As his passengers scrambled to comply, Mark Landi stuffed the top-secret directions to the Virginia outbreak compound into his breast pocket. He raised the binoculars and frowned as he trained his attention on the cars and the moving figures on the road ahead. Then, he slowly swept his gaze to the sides of the road. Next, he turned to scan the road he had just traveled. Finally, he looked above. His heart sank. No sign of the helicopter. He moved the binoculars to take in the scene ahead again.

"What do you see, Dad?" asked Claire.

"The cars are blocking the highway in both directions. On both sides of the cars, it looks as if zombies have been tied to ropes to deter people from getting at the cars."

"That's what it looked like to me, too," agreed Glen. "Why would anyone do that?"

"I can't be certain from this distance, but the zombies appear fresh. I guess that this is a well-planned hijacking operation—and a recent one. Block the highway. Kill motorists, but don't end them. Turn them into zombies to use them as guards. Steal the cars and loot any other useful possessions."

Mark Landi never pulled punches with his team. They all knew what fresh zombies meant. They were the fastest and the most dangerous. But it was the part about killing motorists to doom them to this fate that chilled him the most. *How many people did it take to pull this off? Where were those people now?*

Glen's voice raised an octave as he said, "There's the helicopter!"

KARL Martin never relaxed when he piloted a helicopter. While Jack Crown managed his passengers, he and his copilot scanned non-stop. They had traveled around 200 miles from the outbreak compound. If Mark Landi's Jeep had made sixty miles per hour, he should have covered seventy miles by now and be no more than thirty miles away. They should be closing in on the Jeep in, give or take, ten minutes.

"Look sharp," Karl said to his copilot.

"Always, sir," assured Peter Cook. "We should be seeing them soon."

Collisions were always a risk, especially at low altitudes. Pilots and copilots scanned from before they entered the helicopter until they were safely on the ground. They were always aware of the blind spot under the chopper's nose, especially when climbing or descending.

After the outbreak, air travel plummeted to almost nothing. Most air traffic controllers were fired. The skies were empty except for their chopper. They visually looked out for obstacles, especially an aircraft, however unlikely that was in the post-outbreak world.

Any aircraft that appeared to have no motion relative to their helicopter was probably on a collision course, and if it appeared to increase in size, they were prepared for immediate evasive maneuvers. But they were on the lookout for anything: a drone, birds, humans with weapons, and Mark Landi's Jeep.

They timed their series of short eye movements and scanned around ten degrees for a second at a time. Karl scanned the instrument panel and focused outside the cockpit. They both changed and refocused their gazes at periodic intervals. The skies were clear, and the weather looked stable.

After ten minutes, Peter asked, "See that?"

"Yes," said Karl. "You'd better let Jack and the others know."

Peter toggled the loudspeaker. "Looks like we've got company on the ground. Could be civilians, could be hostiles."

"This looks like a camp," Karl remarked. A long eight-foot-wide swath of grass had been trampled flat. Vehicles had passed through within the past eight hours. The grass hadn't yet dried upright. On one end of the swath were what looked to be an encampment and bunkers. It looked in use but temporarily deserted. On the other end, the highway's lanes were blocked by cars. People oddly milled about. Farther down the highway, he saw a lone vehicle.

"Peter..."

Peter was already scanning the vehicle through his binoculars. "Looks like the Jeep," he confirmed. "Landi stopped well away from the shit show."

This time, Karl toggled the speaker. "Going in for a closer look at a possible hostile compound. Eyes peeled. Guns ready. Chavez, look for an encampment and a makeshift grass road. Drop some smoke grenades for me."

"Will do," responded Major Juan Chavez. "Let them know that we know where they live."

I don't want any collisions with hostile bullets, thought Karl. He went in low for Chavez to send a direct message. *If there is any trouble, the next grenades won't be smoked.* The camp's occupants must be close. They'll see the smoke, and they'll know it's a calling card.

As Karl passed over the grass road, Chavez's voice came over the intercom, "Did you see the fresh cuttings on the underbrush?"

"Yes," responded Karl. "That's why we didn't see off-road vehicles on our approach. They're camouflaged."

Karl ascended and flew toward the Jeep.

Peter peered through binoculars to get a closer look at the cars blocking the road. "Those aren't humans, Karl. Those are zombies. I can see bullet wounds. Lots of them. None of them are headshots. Humans did this."

"Got it," said Karl. "Inform the others."

Peter toggled the speaker. "We've got some bad guys. Zombie makers. Hijackers who shoot victims to kill, but no headshots."

In the rear of the helicopter, Jack turned to Chavez. "You're with me." He turned to two of the soldiers checking their gear. "Bill and Steve, you're with me, too."

Karl intentionally overshot the Jeep and did a one-eighty. The chopper hovered low, inches from the ground, blades spinning. The Jeep was one hundred yards away, between the helicopter and the roadblock.

"SHOOT to maim, shoot to kill, shoot to end," Mark reminded his team. "Get your gear and make your way to the chopper fast."

"Right, coach," said Tom. "Men first. Women behind."

"Ready," said Glen.

"Ready," said Claire and Juliet together.

They opened the doors of the Jeep and piled out. They didn't shut the doors. Their priority was to pay attention to their surroundings, and they might need to make a quick retreat to the Jeep.

Having guns was an element of self-defense, but that was a small part of preparation. One had to know how to use them in a variety of scenarios. A trained group working in concert could thwart a much bigger group. Mark had confidence in his team. But Claire, Glen, and Juliet had never killed a human before. Tom's first human kill was just this morning when he killed Fred. It wasn't the same as a combat situation.

The German, Russian, and Israeli militaries had barred women from combat decades ago. In combat, male troops abandoned tactical objectives to protect female troops. The men tried to protect them from harm. Most of all, they tried to protect them from enemy capture, knowing what the enemy would do to the women as prisoners of war.

Shoot to maim, shoot to kill, and shoot to end was a play Mark had devised should they run into a group of hostile humans. They had drilled with volunteers at the Homewood school compound, but he hoped they wouldn't have to test the strategy when the stakes were life or death. Within seconds, all his plans fell apart.

As Mark and the teens ran toward the chopper, Jack Crown, Juan Chavez, Bill Small, and Steve Markum jumped from the chopper. They ran toward the Jeep to intercept and escort Mark's group to the chopper. Jack left two soldiers behind to protect the open bay doors of the helicopter and the medical team inside.

Jack and his men carried prototype opportunity weapons, custom-designed rifles that replaced the army's M4 and M249 automatic weapons. At first, it looked like an easy mission.

Then came the ambush.

Two foliage-covered vehicles—a car and a paddy wagon—climbed onto the highway, sandwiching themselves between the two running groups.

Six men sprang from the car, and two sprang from the paddy wagon. Ten men sprang from the foliage to confront Mark Landi's group. Another ten men confronted Jack Crown and his three soldiers. The eight men from the vehicles split into two groups and joined their friends. Fourteen men faced Jack and his soldiers, and fourteen faced Mark's group. Mark and the teens were outnumbered by more than two to one. Jack and his men were outnumbered by more than three to one.

Karl and Peter watched helplessly from the helicopter. They couldn't do the kind of precision shooting that would kill only the enemy. Jack and his men were between the chopper and the enemy.

Jack and his men didn't hesitate. They knew the smoke bombs hadn't been a deterrent. These men didn't care that they knew where to find them. That told Jack that trying to intimidate the enemy was a waste of time.

Jack and his men fired the moment the enemy appeared. Jack was as effective with his automatic as he was with a sniper rifle. Six of the men rapidly succumbed to death by Ghost. Chavez culled four. The other four were killed almost instantly by the two soldiers. They advanced to finish with headshots those who didn't die of head wounds in the first place. The ambushers had relied on the element of surprise. They held nothing in reserve. Jack's men were forewarned and well-trained. They slaughtered their ambushers.

Jack looked up, but he couldn't see the Jeep. He signaled his men. One soldier ran to the right. Another to the left. Jack climbed on top of the car.

Chavez faced the helicopter with his back to the foliage-covered vehicles. He stood ready to thwart a surprise flank attack. He also wanted to be sure that none of the bodies between him and the chopper got up again.

"PUT your weapons on the ground!"

"Don't shoot!" Mark shouted.

Mark, Tom, and Glen were in front of Claire and Juliet. The men each raised their empty hands in the air and slowly lowered their weapon hands, crouching to put the weapons on the ground.

"We're unarmed!" shouted Juliet. The girls stood up straight, shoulders back. They had zipped open their shoulder bags and displayed the contents to the ambushers.

It was a maximum distraction play. The ambushers considered the men the maximum threat and focused their attention on the threat. But even wearing their helmets and protective padding, the pretty girls divided the ambushers' attention.

Claire and Juliet drew their pistols from beneath the open shoulder bags and fired at the leaders over the heads of Mark, Tom, and Glen. Claire stood to Juliet's left. Claire shot from the center to her left. Juliet shot from the center to her right. The goal was to shoot to maim—kill, if possible. The spray of bullets damaged the enemy. Four of their attackers dropped in the initial volley. Six were dead or disabled. From the screams of pain, it sounded as if two of the six survived but were badly wounded. That left eight active threats.

Mark, Tom, and Glen hadn't released their weapons. Claire and Juliet dropped down behind them as the men raised their guns and fired. Tom aimed for the middle. Mark aimed to his left, and Glen aimed to his right.

Four more of the enemy went down, and so did Tom. Since Tom was in the middle, the ambushers had assumed he was the leader. The bite plate on his chest had stopped three bullets from piercing his skin. But the protective padding didn't cover every inch of skin. Rapidly flowing blood soaked through the collar of his shirt from a fatal neck wound. He writhed and gasped as he struggled to take his last breaths.

Claire let out a low moan of despair before she and Juliet positioned themselves on either side of Glen and Mark. They searched for targets.

FROM his position on top of the car, Jack Crown saw Tom fall and steadied his automatic rifle. Bill and Steve were in position on opposite sides of the foliage-covered vehicles.

"Our pickups are wearing the helmets," boomed Jack. Shoot the others.

The six remaining ambushers looked over their shoulders in surprise. They had heard the gunfire behind them and assumed their men had won an easy fight. They instantly realized their mistake. Jack and his men dropped three of them with headshots. The other three ran, and they were shot within seconds. Jack dropped his man with a headshot. The other two ambushers were gravely wounded. Bill and Steve closed in and shot them in the head.

Jack held his position on the car's roof. Within a minute or two, ambushers who had been killed without a headshot stood up and walked toward Bill and Steve. The soldiers easily dispatched them with headshots. Meanwhile, Jack waited.

Jack saw the girl turn, step back six feet, and aim her gun at the fallen boy. The man, he guessed Mark Landi, also turned to the boy and aimed his gun. He saw the young man rise. The dead boy was still wearing his football helmet. His eyes looked feral. His lips pulled back in a snarl as he gnashed his teeth. The girl seemed to be saying something. Landi said something to the girl and steadied his gun. Why were they hesitating?

Jack acted. His shot went clean through the helmet, ending the zombie. The boy's helmet was good protection against low-speed impacts and zombie bites, but the high-speed bullet sliced right through it. As the boy's body fell, Jack prayed, "Rest in peace, son."

The girl hovered over the boy. She was crying. Probably her boyfriend. Mark Landi appeared to be saying something to her.

"Move!" roared Jack.

The other two teens ran toward him. Bill and Steve joined them. Mark Landi took the girl by the arm. The pair whirled around and ran toward Jack.

Behind him, Jack heard Chavez's cry an instant before he heard shots fired from Chavez's gun. "Zombies!"

THE noise of the helicopter had attracted the zombies. From their perch in the cockpit, Karl and Peter saw them emerge from the undergrowth. Karl climbed and pivoted ninety degrees to face one side of the road. He descended again, nose close to the side of the road. The tall grass on the side of the road parted from the wind of his blades.

"God help us, it's a horde," Karl said to Peter through tight lips. They strafed the undergrowth, but zombies swarmed the highway. He couldn't strafe in the direction of his men without wounding them. He climbed again and pivoted the chopper 180 degrees. He descended, moving slightly forward, and strafed the other side of the road. He climbed again and flew over the heads of Jack and the others; they were running toward the Jeep.

MOMENTS before, when Chavez raised the alarm, Jack Crown looked over his shoulder and saw Karl's initial climb. He yelled to his men, "Turn around! Fall back to the Jeep!"

The zombies were faster and more agile than Jack expected. It would be impossible to board the helicopter if it set down where it had been hovering. Jack stayed on the car's roof, did a one-eighty, and shot at the heads of the zombies moving toward Juan Chavez. Juan jumped on the car's hood. He and Jack kept shooting, but far too many of the walking dead remained.

"Time to go, Juan," ordered Jack. He and Chavez jumped to the ground on the Jeep side of the car. They hit the ground running.

Clots of zombies were scattered on the road between them and the Jeep. At least it wasn't a horde. These were stragglers, around twenty-five of them, with more emerging from the brush. Mark Landi, the teens, Bill, and Steve were ahead of them.

The runners were flanked by the horde. The underbrush on the sides of the road provided too much cover for hostiles. They had one option—forward, through the stragglers, toward the Jeep.

Karl strafed the sides of the road ahead of the runners. He strafed the highway ahead of them, too. He figured that the zombies he couldn't end would be too chewed up to pose much of a threat. Satisfied with his progress, he turned to Peter. "They don't call this a chopper for nothing."

After strafing, he climbed to make room for those on the ground who were running to the Jeep. The zombies kept coming from the sides of the road, and the horde behind kept moving toward the chopper. Karl flew over the runners and set down, blades spinning, next to the Jeep on the side closest to the roadblock.

Glen shouted, "Headrests!" He ran flat out toward the Jeep ahead and dove inside.

The men were strong enough to butt back the zombies they encountered and shoot them in the head. They shielded the girls who shot at zombies when they found an opening. If they couldn't get a headshot, they tried for the knees to hobble the hostiles. They were careful to avoid wounding anyone else with friendly fire.

Glen emerged from the Jeep with two headrests. The headrests each had two strong steel poles. The poles held the headrests in place when they were attached to a seat. But the poles had another purpose. They were designed to shatter the windshield of the car in case anyone became trapped inside. They were strong enough to pierce a zombie's head. Glen ran back to the group, butting zombies aside as he ran.

"Claire, Juliet," Glenn yelled. He waved the headrests over his head. But he forgot to check high and low around him. He paid for it instantly.

"Behind you, on the ground!" Juliet screamed as a zombie bit an unprotected area on Glen's body, the fleshy area of his left thigh right above the knee and below his thigh guard.

"Damn it!" Glen yelled in fear and rage. He ended the zombie and headshot two more that had closed in on him. He glanced at the bite. Teeth marks tattooed his skin, seeping blood. It didn't hurt much, and he could still run.

The soldiers cleared the way for Glen. He gave one headrest each to Claire and Juliet. The group made fast progress past the Jeep and toward the wide-open bay of the medical rescue helicopter. They were twenty feet away.

The two soldiers, whom Jack had left behind to guard the helicopter, stood in the open door and shot at the heads of approaching zombies. They were careful to avoid shooting their own men. More zombies emerged from the foliage on the side of the road near the helicopter. From his vantage point, Jack saw the medical team join in shooting at the approaching menace.

CLAIRE and Juliet were grateful for the headrests. As they approached the helicopter doorway, they shoved the zombies back with the poles to shoot them from a safer distance. One got so close to Juliet that she had to trap his neck between the poles.

"Shoot it, Claire," Juliet implored.

Claire pushed another zombie away from them. She spun around and shot Juliet's trapped zombie in the head.

The men pushed the zombies away from the chopper door and held them at bay. They had a rhythm of pushing followed by headshots. A zombie closed in on Jack. Mark whacked it in the mouth with his padded arm and shot it in the head.

The medical team retreated further into the chopper. The two soldiers inside the chopper stood in the doorway, firing at zombies around the men on the ground.

Claire grabbed Juliet's arm. "They've created an opening for us. Run for it!"

A soldier sprang from the chopper door to help Claire and Juliet scramble inside. When they were safely onboard, he activated the megaphone. "We've got the girls. All aboard!" He resumed shooting at zombies to give the men as much cover as possible.

A cluster of highway zombies caught up to Jack's group, and more came from the undergrowth, attracted by the chopper's sounds. Despite their efforts, the small perimeter they had created was collapsing. They were six feet from the door.

Jack turned to Mark and Glen. "Get in the chopper," he bellowed.

Mark and Glen turned and took a running jump inside.

Jack, Chavez, Bill, and Steve formed a tight concave semicircle and moved slowly back toward the door. They shoved and shot the zombies closest to them while the two soldiers inside the chopper shot over their heads at the zombies just outside their reach.

They were at the chopper's door. "Steve and Bill, break away," Jack commanded.

Steve and Bill leaped on board the chopper.

Jack turned to Chavez. "Together. Now."

They bounded inside and secured the door.

Steve used the intercom. "Cargo is loaded. We're all on board."

Karl ascended rapidly and headed toward the Virginia outbreak compound at full speed. He wanted to put distance between them and that hellish place.

JACK turned to the passengers. "I think it's time we introduced ourselves, and I want to see the young man who's been bitten."

They quickly went through the introductions.

"Glen, let me have a look at that bite," Jack said.

Glen looked at the medical team in white coats and then looked at Jack in surprise.

"He's a doctor. A good one," Chavez clarified. He shed his gear and opened his shirt. "Stitched me up in Afghanistan. I was sliced with a knife. Missed my organs. Miracle I lived. Today, you can barely see the scar."

Glen forgot his injury as he examined Chavez's taut torso. "Nice six-pack. I wish I were that ripped. The scar is almost invisible."

Juliet caught Claire's eye. She looked at Chavez's torso and back at Claire. She raised an eyebrow, and her dark eyes twinkled. "Diet Coke break," she whispered.

The corners of Claire's lips moved up. She tossed back her long, auburn hair and suppressed a giggle.

Mark Landi was glad to see that the girls had enough spirit left to share a joke. He worried about Claire. She wasn't injured on the outside, but she had taken a brutal beating today, nonetheless. He moved to Glen's side.

"Take off your gear and lay on your stomach," instructed Jack.

Jack cleaned up as best he could, disinfected his hands, donned a mask and scrubs, disinfected his hands again, and put on gloves.

While Jack prepared, a medic removed Glen's body padding and set his weapons to the side. Glen rolled onto his stomach. The medic cut away the fabric of the leg of Glen's pants and cleaned the entire leg except for the wound.

"Let me see what we've got." Jack examined the wound and gently touched it around the edges. The flesh around the margins of the bite was red and puffy. Based on what he knew about Z-Factor, within a couple of hours, it would be a suppurating wound. After that, things would progress rapidly in the wrong direction. Jack carefully and thoroughly cleaned the wound and dressed it. As he worked, he spoke to Glen to put him at ease.

"Remind me of your name, son." Jack remembered, but he wanted to engage Glen and check his lucidity.

"Glen Anderson."

"Do you have any allergies, Glen?"

"No."

"No allergies to antibiotics? Are you sure?"

"No allergies that I know of."

Jack turned to the medic who had assisted earlier. "Give him the standard dose injection of amoxicillin/clavulanate when I'm done."

Jack turned back to Glen. "How old are you?"

"Seventeen." His voice quavered.

Jack looked at Glen's face. Glen fought like a man. He was brave and never hesitated when fighting off the threat. He was a powerfully built teenager but still no match for a mature, trained soldier. Lying on the cot with a fresh zombie bite and no way to fight back, he looked like a frightened boy. That's because he was.

"You showed the presence of mind to think of the smashing power of the Jeep's headrests. Smart thinking," remarked Jack.

"My father died in a car accident. The people who hit my dad were trapped in their car. The driver was killed and turned into a zombie. I've often thought about what I'd do if I were trapped in a car with a zombie and had no access to a weapon."

"You left the group..."

"I didn't break tactical training if that's what you mean. Our objective was to protect Claire and Coach Landi. They're hoping for a possible cure. That's why Tom Peters took the middle position. He drew fire away from Coach Landi and Claire."

Claire and Juliet were riveted by Glen's words. Tears coursed down their cheeks.

"When was your last tetanus shot, Glen?"

Glen looked at Coach Landi as he answered Jack's question. "A couple of months ago. We all had them."

Mark nodded. "That's right. We brought everyone's shots and immunizations up to date. Everyone practices good hygiene, eats properly, and sticks to an exercise, study, play, and sleep schedule."

"Because of the outbreak?" Jack asked.

"Bringing immunizations up to date was due to the outbreak. It was a wake-up call. The rest is just good parenting. Someone has to teach discipline to the young."

Jack smiled beneath his mask. "We're always in need of refresher courses."

Jack said to Glen, "You can get up now. We're almost home. We'll monitor you round the clock and make sure you get the very best of care."

Glen sat up and nodded glumly.

Jack turned to Mark. "Next."

Mark took off his shirt while Jack changed his gloves.

Jack examined Mark's triceps. "Good job with the cleaning and dressing. Who did it?"

"My colleague at the Homewood compound."

"Does this hurt?" Jack applied gentle pressure around six inches from the bite.

"No."

"Tell me when it does." Jack slowly worked inwards toward the bite.

"That feels a little tender."

"That's what I would expect with a normal wound. It appears to be healing well. I'm done for now. We'll know more when we've had a chance to run tests."

Jack straightened up and raised his voice. "Grab something to eat everybody. We have a short ride, and we stocked up for five days, just in case. Let's make a dent in it."

"HOW is your daughter holding up?" Jack nodded in Claire's direction. She sat with Juliet off to the side. Both girls had eaten and were talking in a low voice. They looked subdued and their previous banter was gone.

"In the past twenty-four hours, she fought off a zombie attack, saw me get bitten, nearly shot me thinking I was a zombie, learned she may or may not have the key to a Z-Factor cure, was nearly killed by a looter who she thought was a friend, watched her boyfriend shoot the looter in the head, said goodbye to her home and friends, engaged in a shoot-out with ambushers, watched her boyfriend die, watched him ended, fought of a zombie swarm, and watched a good friend get bitten. I'd say my daughter's holding herself together with Scotch tape and string."

"I shot her boyfriend. The two of you hesitated."

"I'm glad you did. We were saying our goodbyes to Tom. I didn't want Claire to have the trauma of ending him, but I wasn't keen to give her the memory of me ending Tom."

For the first time, Mark took Jack's measure. They stood eye to eye at six feet four inches. Mark knew he was powerfully built and in good shape, but Jack was even more toned. Jack was accomplished. A doctor, a soldier, a crack shot. He figured Jack was about ten years younger, in his early thirties, the peak of his manhood.

"You were on the roof of the car, weren't you? That was quite a shot."

Jack shrugged. "Lots of practice."

"You're quite the package, Dr. Crown."

Jack looked around at his men. "We all are. That's why we were chosen for the Outbreak Compound. But you're no slouch yourself. We're delighted to have you."

"My daughter needs to keep busy. We all need something to do." He looked over to Glen who was talking to Chavez. "Except Glen," he said ruefully. "They are just kids. I was supposed to protect them; they weren't supposed to protect me."

"You didn't fail them. I couldn't have done better in those circumstances. No one could have."

"I'll be replaying it in my mind for a long time."

It was Jack's turn to take Mark's measure. Early forties. Smart. Resourceful. Healthy. Athletic. Devoted father. A good man in a storm. There was a lot to like about Mark Landi.

"When we get to the compound, we'll find you something to do. Something you'll like doing. You're a chemistry teacher, right? And you're good with teens. That's obvious. We'll keep you very busy when we aren't running tests."

The intercom broke in to relay Karl's cheerful voice. "We're home. Prepare for landing. It's 12:45 p.m. We have perfect weather at the Outbreak Compound."

*****

GLEN reported directly to the medical bay. Claire, Juliet, and Mark showered and changed. They were given clean fatigues and handed over their soiled clothing for laundering. Then they reported to the medical bay for blood tests and thorough physicals. Mark donated blood. After that, Steve gave them a two-hour tour of the compound, ending with the dining hall at 7:00 p.m.

"Time for dinner," announced Steve. "Let's see what's on the menu." He grabbed a paper printout at the entrance. "Mixed salad, chicken l 'orange, asparagus, sweet potato fries, and sourdough bread. Raspberries and chocolate chip cookies for dessert."

Bill and Chavez joined them for dinner to make a table of six.

"Jack and his wife, Dr. Grace Crown, are dining in the medical bay. Jack thought you might find familiar faces easier for your first dinner," Chavez explained. "We'll all report to the medical bay at ten o'clock for an update on Glen."

After dinner, they stopped into a recreation room where soldiers and their wives put on a jam fest. Mark had to admit there were some decent musicians in this compound. Jack was right. Everyone here brought a variety of accomplishments to the table.

They arrived at the medical bay at ten on the dot. An orderly showed them into a room with a small conference table. The orderly placed a carafe of water with glasses in the middle of the table and left the room.

They had just sat down when Jack entered the room with another tall man. He was six feet three inches, an inch shorter than Jack, and thinner, less muscular. Jack began, "This is Dr. Benjamin Lieber. He's the best mind in this field. He's here to bring you up to date." Jack introduced each of the newcomers in turn before Ben proceeded.

Ben cleared his throat and took a sip of water. "We collected plasma from Coach Mark Landi earlier this afternoon. He was a match with Glen Anderson. We're trying convalescent plasma therapy. For those of you who haven't heard of it before, the treatment was first used in the 1918 flu pandemic. Since then, it has been used with mixed success to treat H1N1, Ebola, and other viral diseases."

"I've heard of it," acknowledged Claire. "We all have. It's one of the first things my father taught us after the outbreak. The only problem was no one we knew of had antibodies."

"Your father does. Your results show that you do, too."

"How is Glen?" asked Juliet.

"His wound looks better than when he arrived. The swelling has subsided. He doesn't have a fever. He feels fine, and he's in good spirits. But I don't want to give you false hope. We're monitoring him carefully. You can say goodnight to him if you wish."

They went as a group to see Glen. Claire noticed a new face in Glen's room. A wiry, green-eyed, young man with light brown hair stood beside Glen's bed. He was around six feet tall and carried himself as if he were Mr. Spock.

Juliet took Glen's hand. "How are you feeling?"

"You can't get rid of me that easily. I caught that Diet Coke crack."

Juliet blushed and laughed. "Guilty."

Glen's face grew serious. "I hope this works."

"We all hope it works," Ben agreed. He gestured to the boy standing next to Glen's bed. "This is my son, Carl. Since you arrived, he's been scanning for reports of hordes. It's grim. Even if the plasma works, the treatment is too granular. The Landis can't supply plasma for the world. We need to develop solutions for mass distribution. Humans are under siege."

"Our excursion today didn't go unnoticed," added Jack. Citizen band radio operators spotted our chopper. Our location is a secret for now, but they saw the general direction we were flying. It sounds as if they don't have much to go on, but we can't assume that we'll be left alone."

"At least we have something we didn't have yesterday," said Carl.

"What's that?" asked Claire.

Carl turned to her and flashed a smile. "Hope."

JACK Crown said nothing. Zombies have a sole goal: human flesh. Even if we find a cure for the living, *will we survive?*

SPECIAL EXCERPT FROM ZOMBIE APOCALYPSE 2: WILDFIRE

Fog of War

Month Four of the Z-Factor Outbreak

Friday 0515

Fresh blood turned the front of Tom's white shirt bright red. Tom Peters drew enemy fire away from his companions: Mark "Coach" Landi, Claire Landi, his 17-year-old daughter, and teenagers Juliet Romero and Glen Anderson. The boy fell. No one could survive that volley. Yet Tom Peters soon rose from a prone position. He gnashed his teeth as he approached Claire and Mark Landi.

"Pause the video clip," commanded Colonel Jack Crown, M.D.

Body cameras with zoom lenses captured details that the soldiers who took part in yesterday's away mission hadn't noticed in real time. Tom's blood-soaked shirt was a red badge of courage. Tom died a hero's death. He was barely seventeen.

"Continue," said Jack.

The next angle was slow-motion footage from Jack's body camera. Jack was atop a car two hundred yards away. Tom Peters had been handsome. Jack hadn't noticed as he aimed at the snarling zombie that, just seconds before, had been a strong, healthy young man.

Jack took a clean sniper shot at Tom's head. The high-speed bullet hit the teen's forehead, tore through his skull, and shattered his football helmet. Tom's head exploded in a red mist.

We all die, thought Jack. But could he have saved Tom Peters or at least given the boy better odds?

Yes. It was obvious now. Why wasn't it obvious yesterday? Jack knew it wasn't just the fog of war. He was following orders. The orders had to change.

Special Excerpt

*****

Mark Landi and his daughter carried rare genes. They were immune to the Z-Factor virus. Yesterday, Mark Landi's party left their compound in Homewood to make the 300-mile journey to the Outbreak Compound. The other teens volunteered to go on the drive with Mark and Claire Landi. Mark was a football coach and their high school chemistry teacher.

Jack's team rendezvoused with them in a helicopter near the halfway mark. The mission was well worth the risk of exposing the location of the Outbreak Compound.

As Jack's team exited the helicopter and approached Landi's car, ambushers attacked. During the firefight, the ambushers shot and killed Tom Peters. Jack ended Tom with a rifle shot to the head.

A zombie horde attacked them. In the melee, a zombie bit Glen Anderson. They fought their way back to the helicopter and spirited Glen to the Outbreak Compound. The medical team injected Glen with Mark Landi's antibodies, and Glen's condition was improving.

*****

"Replay our arrival at the rendezvous," commanded Jack.

Jack led yesterday's mission with seven volunteers: Major Juan Chavez, Lieutenants Steve Markum, Karl "Kay" Martin, Peter Cook, Bill Small, Ronny Hanes, and Dusty Rhodes. They were part of the Outbreak Compound's cadre of soldiers.

At thirty-three, Jack already had a lifetime of education and broad combat experience. Juan Chavez was a year his junior. Jack's troops were twenty-six years old and at least six feet two inches tall. They exceeded General Gary Markum's sky-high requirements for intelligence scores, psychological profiles, and other unique characteristics.

Lt. Steve Markum's deft fingers tapped the keyboard as he skillfully cycled the software and adjusted the video. "Here it is, sir, in slow motion." Steve pressed a key to project his screen's display on the opposite wall.

Jack ran his right hand through his dark, loose curls. His deep blue eyes scanned the screen. A small muscle throbbed at the side of his jaw. He edged forward on his chair.

Special Excerpt

The footage began when the helicopter flew over the ambushers' roadblock. Cars zigzagged across the highway, blocking both lanes. Zombies, tied to the fenders, flayed their limbs. Some had ropes around their waists, others around their necks. Their lips pulled back from their gums. They chomped their teeth at the air. Lifeless bodies jerked, stumbled, and collided. But that wasn't the most disturbing part.

Steve Markum froze the video. He gazed at the life-sized projected image. Then he swiftly looked away. He closed his eyes, bowed his head, and rubbed the muscles between his eyebrows with his thumb and forefinger.

All the zombies had chest wounds. The women, girls, and young boys were only partially clothed. Blood and bruises covered the men's faces. Pre-mortem injuries. The ambushers beat the men when they tried to defend the women and children.

The ambushers hadn't merely created zombies. The ambushers humiliated, demoralized, and tortured their captives before they murdered them. The ambushers used their captives' zombified bodies to terrorize any newcomer they snared.

Peter Cook, the helicopter's copilot and look-out, tapped Steve Markum's upper arm. "There it is. That's what I saw through the binoculars."

Bill Small and Ronny Hanes stood with their arms crossed, glaring at the screen. At six feet two inches, they were the same height as Dusty Rhodes. Dusty furiously twisted the Rubik's Cube, which he habitually scrambled and solved several times a day.

Ronny clicked his tongue in disgust. Ronny's commanding officer said during his Iraq deployment that he slept with one eye open. Some of the men were afraid of him. In those days, Ronny wore a gold stud in his left ear and a headband torn from an old camouflage shirt. His shoulder-length hair covered a jagged scar on the side of his face.

Today, Ronny sported a trim military cut with his scar in full view. The earring was gone. Somehow, he looked even more dangerous than he had during deployment. He always carried at least a gun and a knife. Ronny was hyper-alert, yet he was as even-tempered as any of the other men.

Kay Martin, the helicopter's pilot, took in a sharp breath. "Those monsters. I'm glad we killed them." His quick-moving brown eyes took in the images. His chestnut brown hair was even with the blond head of his first officer and copilot, Peter Cook.

"I'm glad, too," said Peter. His blue eyes were riveted to the screen. His face looked like a thundercloud. His m

"Yes, Peter," said Jack Crown. "The rest of us didn't see those details in real-time. It was enough that they killed those people, but this makes it even more heinous."

Peter Cook wheeled around to face him. Jack compressed his lips into a straight line. His face showed determination. Peter recognized that look. *Colonel Crown has something up his sleeve.*

Out of the corner of his eye, Peter saw General Gary Markum, Commander of the Outbreak Compound, and a shorter man, Captain Arthur Barton, M.D., the compound's psychiatrist. They stood off to the side, speaking in such low tones that the other men couldn't overhear their conversation.

At five feet eleven inches, Dr. Arthur Barton was the only man in the room under six feet two inches tall. The forty-eight-year-old was the most talented military psychiatrist in the U.S. armed forces.

General Markum was in his late fifties but still fit enough to achieve top scores when he topped up training. The Outbreak Compound was the culmination of more than seventy years of planning by Markum and his predecessors.

Markum handpicked every member of his team, just as he had been chosen when he was a young man. Every year, he refreshed a list of troops targeting those who were twenty-six years old. For decades, he dropped names off the list as the troops aged out. He added new names, ready for the day the young men were needed to populate the Outbreak Compound.

He identified mentally and physically healthy children with a minimum intelligence quotient of 140, some much higher. If necessary, the government intervened to nurture their education and monitor their progress. Markum dropped those who couldn't meet a series of ongoing challenges.

The government offered the chosen children military academy scholarships. Markum steered the children to a special training program. He invited the top eighteen-year-olds to join the military.

Special Excerpt

They received more specialized training and specific combat duty. Markum invited the best performers to join a special reserve team in case a national emergency required him to activate the Outbreak Protocol. That time arrived four months ago when the Z-Factor virus infected the entire human race.

General Markum took the podium. He stood before the screen, erect, a commanding presence. Every eye was upon him.

"Colonel Crown," said Markum, looking at Jack, "Dr. Barton and I agree with your medical and military assessment."

Jack stood motionless. A slight nod of his head acknowledged Markum's words.

"The chaplain will say a memorial mass for Tom Peters at 0700. Everyone who can take time from his duties is welcome to attend." Markum knew every man in the compound who wasn't on duty would attend the service for the fallen young hero.

Markum looked down at the laptop on the podium and tapped a few keys. "I just sent you an electronic copy of a document," said Markum. "You've read it before. Read it again. The title is 'Operation Wildfire.'"

The room fell silent.

"Questions?" asked General Markum

"Sir!" said Dusty Rhodes. His Rubik's Cube clattered to the floor. "I'd like to request leave to visit Gregg's Farm."

A knowing laugh escaped from Ronny Hanes and Bill Small.

General Markum kept his face neutral. "Gregg's Farm? Do you mean our experimental self-sustaining pilot farm run by a retired colonel? Do you want to check up on new energy storage developments?"

"Sir, General Markum, sir," said Dusty, "I'd like to request personal leave, sir."

"That personal leave wouldn't be female and about twenty-two, would it, Lieutenant Rhodes?"

"Yes, sir! I believe that's about right, sir!" Dusty Rhodes grinned from ear to ear.

General Markum allowed himself the hint of a smile. He nodded to Rhodes. Then he nodded at Colonel Jack Crown, M.D., glanced at his watch, and strode from the room.

*****

Special Excerpt

Jack moved to the middle of the room with the easy stride of a well-trained athlete. If he were a professional athlete, sports psychologists would describe his calm and control as the iceberg profile.

"You already know what Wildfire means. We will retrain to have a modified combat mindset. Our paramount objective is to protect the Outbreak Compound and its satellites. We will expand to make room for your future wives and future nuclear families. Our objective is not to protect random civilians nor to give them the benefit of the doubt. Our new bias is to protect our people. Our mission is to survive."

"Will the other body cam and helicopter camera footage be ready for our 0800 meeting?" Jack asked Lieutenant Steve Markum.

"Affirmative, sir. It's ready for prime time," replied Steve. A wisp of Steve Markum's light brown hair fell to his forehead as he leaned closer to his computer screen. "We worked on it yesterday afternoon. We'll recheck everything before the 0800 assembly, but yes, it's ready now."

"Good," was all Jack said.

"I don't know how we could have had a better outcome." Steve brushed away a bead of sweat traveling toward his intense steel-grey eyes. He looked down and busied himself with his equipment.

Jack made a mental note to have Steve take some time off. Steve was General Markum's son. He was qualified, part of the elite group, and eligible to be here. He was here on merit. Steve sometimes pushed himself too hard to make it clear nepotism wasn't a factor.

"We can all learn something from this cluster," Jack said.

Special Excerpt

The Alexandria Massacre

The official government narrative was a lie. During the first days of the Z-Factor outbreak, the media claimed it was a conspiracy theory.

Disinformation is government propaganda designed to mislead one's enemies. Russia perfected it. China adopted it. The USA's frightened government used it against its citizens during the Z-Factor apocalypse.

Yuri Bezmenov, a KGB spy who defected in the 1970s, stated that the goal of all such propaganda is to "change the perception of reality of every American to such an extent that despite the abundance of information, no one is able to come to sensible conclusions in the interest of defending themselves, their families, their community, and their country."

A retired major who taught Information Operations at the National Defense Intelligence College explained to his class:

> Conspiracy theories are fun and dangerous.

There are four types of conspiracy theories. First, you have the kooks, such as the flat earthers.

Operation INFEKTION, is a second type of conspiracy theory. Russia's KGB claimed the USA invented AIDS as a biological warfare weapon. Russia's goal was to cause dissension in the U.S. and discredit America in the eyes of the world.

A third type of conspiracy theory is designed to discredit an argument, discredit an accusation, or discredit a group. For example, a stripper hired for a party falsely accused three students on Duke University's lacrosse team of rape. The boys were no angels, but neither was the stripper, and the boys weren't rapists. Mainstream media smeared the entire team, along with white male college students in general. The media flooded the zone with accusations, but the retractions got almost no airtime.

The fourth type is an actual conspiracy.

Special Excerpt

Politicians conspired against the people who voted for them. They told lie after lie in a bid to stay in power because power meant control of dwindling resources.

*****

The USA fell the way Rome fell. It had grown soft and stupid. Actors, comedians, rap singers, and athletes were national celebrities. None of them had useful skills in the world after Z-Factor, except for some of the athletes.

Before Z-Factor, playing victim became a strategy to claim moral superiority. Manufacturing hate crimes became a lucrative full-time job for the grifter class. Victim organizations asked for contributions to fight "injustice." Their founders lived in mansions. Yet those whom the founders claimed to champion were lucky to get these so-called advocates to pay for a meal.

Victim status was a social advantage before the Z-Factor virus. Now, it was a huge liability. No one wanted or needed victims who claimed that historical "oppressors" were the ancestors of undeserving people. These "victims" were, in fact, toxic aggressors.

Survivors were skeptical that professional victims would pull their own weight. Healthy people suspected the victim-grifters would be divisive crybullies, always looking for an angle for their own benefit at the expense of an imaginary "oppressor."

Z-Factor revealed something important to humanity. People need to believe that their way of life matters. People need to be convinced that lives are worth saving. It is the key to survival.

Smart people quickly realized everyone was in a fight for their lives. New social groups formed. They prized loyalty, not selfish victims who manufactured injustices, looking to blame others for their lack of resources.

Women learned what they should have known from human history. When women became more influential in public life, it was often associated with national decline.

Panic, fear, and confusion gripped Americans. Streets were violent and unsafe for unescorted women. Women learned that martial arts weren't much good when they were set upon by more than one man or a man who was just as skilled.

Radical feminists who had slandered men with claims of "toxic masculinity" became pariahs before they changed their discordant tune. They wailed that men didn't leap into the fray to defend women from predators. The woke culture collapsed overnight.

Both men and women wanted to be with strong men of solid character whom other strong men would willingly follow. Communities circled the wagons to protect families.

Before most of the mainstream media's microphones went dead, one local man summed up the new street reality. "Why should I put my life on the line for random strangers who may be setting me up for a mugging? My job is to make it home in one piece to protect my family and the people I know and love. Today, it's all about family, your neighbors, whom you know, and whom you trust. Unity is our strength."

Men with leadership skills were in short supply. Town councils invited men who knew how to fight and find food to resettle in struggling towns. People deposed mediocre bureaucrats. A great resorting of terrified human society was underway.

*****

Six days after the Z-Factor outbreak, the president ordered army combat veterans to disperse a horde of infected protesters who planned to gather in Market Square near City Hall in Alexandria, Virginia. The soldiers had already spent two horrific days fighting off zombies in Washington, D.C.

Their commanding officers told them that the infected protesters were anarchists. The infected had nothing left to lose. The infected were determined to rush the capitol and infect everyone inside after they turned.

But the protesters were not infected. The protesters showed up in support of the government. They thought they were protesting a wild conspiracy theory about the Z-Factor virus. They thought news about zombies was a hoax designed to undermine elected officials. None of the protesters was armed.

Protesters filled the red brick plaza that led to City Hall. Fountains spouted water in a large shallow square pool. Wide lanes paved with red brick surrounded the pool. The protesters spilled onto the stairs and the square below.

Soldiers arrived on foot, in vehicles, and on horseback. They surrounded the courtyard. Others positioned themselves around the square below. They formed a fighting force four deep.

The soldiers herded the protesters in a pincer move, driving them up to the courtyard and packing them in. They began slaughtering protesters at the edge of the crowd. Those in the middle were so crushed that they couldn't fight. The troops shot protesters and sabered them through the head.

Afterward, three hundred forty-seven corpses lay on the courtyard's blood-soaked brick paths.

You've finished. Before you go…

Tweet/share that you finished this book.

Write a brief customer review on Amazon or your favorite site for book lovers.

Give *Zombie Apocalypse: The Origin* as a gift to your favorite horror fan!

Follow Michael K. Clancy on Amazon and check for new releases.

Books by Michael K. Clancy

Zombie Apocalypse: The Origin

Zombie Apocalypse 2: WILDFIRE

Zombie Apocalypse 3: Ghost Territory

Check Amazon for updates on new releases.

Fiction Books via Lyons McNamara

FICTION - MYSTERY

Archangels: Rise of the Jesuits
By Janet M. Tavakoli

"Conspiracies within conspiracies, a fast-paced thriller"
—*Publisher's Weekly*

About Michael K. Clancy

Michael K. Clancy has a degree in chemical engineering and is an avid reader of nonfiction science books and journals.

Sign up for updates on Michael's new books by sending an email with your name and email address to: Michaelclancy74@gmail.com

Follow Michael K. Clancy on Twitter @z_factor1

Made in the USA
Middletown, DE
25 March 2025

73267217R00150